DIGI
TUS
INDIE PUBLISHERS

Contrapuntos X

❖

OESTE

Cristina Rentería Garita, ed.

EDITORES INDEPENDIENTES
Monterey, CA

Diseño · *Design:* Arturo Torres, Ángel M. Rañales.

Editors: Marcos Pico Rentería, Ángel M. Rañales
Guest Editor: Cristina Rentería Garita
Preparación de manuscrito preliminar: Miguel Ángel Albujar

First print edition: 2024

ISBN Digitus Indie Publishers: 978-0-9982539-7-8

ISSN 2 4 7 2 - 2 0 6 5 (print)
ISSN 2 4 7 2 - 2 0 7 3 (online)
www.digitusindie.com

ÍNDICE
CONTENTS

NOTA EDITORIAL

Un destacado erudito de las letras por nombre Jorge Luis instruía en sus lecciones sobre el propósito de la lectura. Simplemente, felicidad. En la edición que recopila varias de sus ponencias hacia el final de su vida, concretamente la grandiosa *Borges oral*, el autor se encargaba de puntualizar el valor de las letras, esa inmortalidad cósmica en la que se acoge la palabra, en la que se refugia el ser humano. Es esta máxima la que solicitamos enfrentar y cumplir aquí.

Los editores y el equipo editorial de Digitus Indie Publishers se complacen en presentar el segundo volumen de nuestra edición de aniversario, la ansiada décima. Siendo *Contrapuntos X: East* la primera travesía, se hace aquí entrega de la segunda, *Contrapuntos X: West.* Ambas ediciones pugnan amistosamente por ofrecer una panorámica literaria del territorio estadounidense con voces en lengua española e inglesa. Es esta nueva edición la pieza conclusiva de un aniversario que hemos abrazado con una ilusión gentilmente desmedida y que esperamos que el lector saboree en las páginas que siguen. Es en este sentido nuestra simple aportación a una sofisticación literaria a la que autores y autoras, editores y editoras, se han dedicado apasionada y voluntariamente en estos dos años que nos han visto crecer.

Contrapuntos X: West quiere proponerse como un camino hacia el encuentro. Esta pequeña introducción no desvelará cumplido alguno. Solamente entreabrimos en esta nota una puerta que espera ser traspasada con curiosidad y sin atenuantes. No hay aquí nombres de autores, no títulos ni visiones perspicaces por adelantado. Únicamente se agradece a la editora invitada de esta edición, Cristina Rentería Garita, por su labor en el proceso editorial para que estas letras lleguen a buen puerto, a las manos de los lectores y las imaginaciones de sus veredictos.

Como homenaje a la edición anterior y como justa continuación, *Contrapuntos X: West* se consigna a una sección poética jubilosa y suculenta, sorpresiva pero nunca conclusiva, como buena poética. La ficción le continúa con una selección variopinta y bien sazonada, apetitosa, seguida de la ya notoria no-ficción que caracteriza a las letras modernas. Siendo esta una edición accesoria, si se permite, "Rutas paralelas" sirve de nuevo de corolario, asumiendo un desvío geográfico y esta vez asimismo de cierta transfiguración literaria.

Cerramos estas verbas con un guiño a esa circularidad tan característica de la creación borgiana. Que el territorio de la palabra escrita incite a la imaginación del lector a viajar, a divagar, a perderse, y que sea infinitamente.

los editores
en Monterey y Augusta

POESÍA

LENGUAJE, REFLEXIÓN Y RESISTENCIA

Como mexicana fuera de su entorno natal, formar parte de *Contrapuntos X: Oeste* ha sido, sin duda, una experiencia muy emotiva. Conocer las obras de hombres y mujeres que, desde su lugar en el mundo, observan, abstraen y siguen su pulsión de crear allí donde, quizá, se empieza una nueva vida, ha sido, a su vez, reconocer que los creadores somos artífices conjuntos de un enorme acto de resistencia.

Porque la creación, desde el mismo momento que comienza a gestarse ya está dentro de la larga carrera por sobrevivir. En literatura, si hablamos de poesía, sobre todo, el tiempo, se añade a la ecuación, y va desechando todo aquello innecesario; sin impaciencias, no admite versos flojos.

El trabajo de cada uno de los creadores y creadoras que aquí se presentan, esboza un amplio y compartido escenario de resistencias. Muestra realidades sociales no sólo desde una perspectiva antropológica, sino también desde la fuerza emotiva de la impronta o la realidad, por cruda que sea; del volver a un lugar de recuerdos y sensaciones; de hacerlo con los ojos adaptados del hoy. Estos autores y autoras confrontan su identidad dentro de una región enorme y distinta, dejándonos poemas que son estampas personales y, si mirados en conjunto, una aproximación de cómo son aquellos y aquellas que, desde el idioma anfitrión y, en muchos casos, con la mente formada en español, crean en el oeste de Estados Unidos.

Dado que mi labor ha sido reconocer un punto de vista a partir de rasgos comunes, **Carlos Ponce Meléndez** marca la hoja de intenciones. Muestra la experiencia de aprender y aprehender desde el lenguaje y sus representaciones, desde el lugar al que se accede dentro de los valores de una sociedad, donde la soledad, por el simple hecho de ser ajeno espectador, se convierte en una compañera de trayecto.

Jesús Cortez, quien se reconoce como indocumentado de raíces mexicanas, pero de California, tiene una intención eminentemente política. Dibuja imágenes en sepia en las que los verbos intentar y adaptarse son una constante de su propio sino.

Michael Manerowski, a través de la voz en español de la traductora Katherine Adcock, crea escenarios abstractos, casi oníricos, pero, de igual manera, densos, que dejan una pesada sensación de soledad y ajenitud allá donde los haga.

Jennifer Rathbun juega con del bilingüismo, con su capacidad de organizar las ideas, los conceptos, las emociones. Sabe que el idioma cincela y filtra, mientras que su lenguaje, afianza y matiza; que corazón significa heart, pero que no suenan de la misma manera. Por eso, quizá, Rathbun nos ofrece poemas mestizos, con México colándose entre cada letra.

LR Cunningham busca en el español una herramienta de expresión particular para mostrarnos su experiencia como observadora del entorno y las situaciones. En inglés, nos deja un poema personal, emotivo y, como los demás de esta selección, agudo en información sobre la sociedad en que se gesta.

Lisandra Pérez ofrece poemas llenos de impronta, de madres y tradiciones, de sensaciones y, también, de experiencia de adaptación. La conquista del nuevo idioma se mezcla con la travesía de no olvidar los propios orígenes, de saber que del otro lado de la frontera está México y que a la tierra prometida se ha llegado a pie.

Colin Ian Jeffery muestra poemas más narrativos en los que, por un lado, la naturaleza, la ley del más fuerte, siempre se impone mientras, por el otro, reflexiona sobre su lugar en el mundo y la idea de posteridad. Contrasta con el tono de la selección, pero por ello, justamente, permite vislumbrar los intereses y matices de los creadores dentro de una misma región.

Finalmente, **Jorge Manzanilla Pérez** presenta poemas duros llenos historia, de pasado, de memoria y de realidad. No habla de un lugar del que se eligen los colores o el folclore, sino del que se huye para resistir y sobrevivir: el de la violencia macerada por siglos, el de las despedidas y el de la tristeza endurecida. México se lleva en la espalda, no en el imaginario.

Así, bienvenidos a la selección de poesía de *Contrapuntos X: West*. En ella queda de manifiesto que el hilo conductor de estos y estas poetas, no sólo es el territorio que les ha tocado compartir sino, y de manera más significativa, cómo se sienten acogidos por él en un constante pendular entre su historia personal, sus raíces y su imaginario, heredado, o no, donde el lenguaje se corona como la más profunda y rebelde forma de expresión, reflexión y resistencia.

HOW TO PRONOUNCE IN ENGLISH IN AMERICA

Carlos Ponce Menéndez

IF YOUR FIRST language is not English
You need to learn 56 phonograms
And a few hundred exceptions.
It means countless ways to pronounce "a," "e"
All the other vowels, most consonants
And many combinations between them.

Americans have a very special pronunciation
Therefore, follow the next rules if you want
To pass for an American native.

First rule; when you say money
You need to prolong the "y," capturing the word
As if this were the most important word in the world.
By contrast if you say poor,
Try to expel the air in the "oo" as far as you can
Ejecting the spirit of the word.

Second rule; to say democracy, pretend.
Simulate to use a strong K instead of the cr.
If it is too difficult, at least make believe, fooling the people.
Very different is the pronunciation of foreign,
Now, you must eat as many letters as you can,
Don't worry about its soul, it is not an original America.

Third rule; when saying freedom use the "e"
As the "i" in libertine. Here you can take
Some latitude and do as you want.

In the case of the word sex
You have to be fast and to the point.
Aim to the X. There is not case in loosing time
As when you say love. That takes too much time.

Finally, when you pronounce "English"
Don't forget to use the "i" instead of the "E", Inglish.
It's not hard to do it if you remember that it is the same
"i" of "I" (I, me, me first, and only me).
"I" as in individual and egocentriiiic.
If you learn these basic rules, you'll
Be suited to speak American.

EL AUTOBÚS

Carlos Ponce Menéndez

EN UNA NOCHE muy fría me siento en una banca de madera castigada
con Graffiti a esperar el autobús de la ruta setenta y seis.
Cuando lo veo venir siento un calorcillo en mi corazón,
Anticipo la calidez del viaje en el intestino del trasporte urbano.

Con unas cuantas monedas adquiero el derecho
A viajar por cerca de cuarenta millas, la ruta obrera.
Solo otros tres pasajeros comparten mi destino
Cada uno por su lado y el chofer con su cara de cansado.

La temperatura no es muy diferente a la de la calle
Pero cualquier mejora se agradece
Y con ello escojo un asiento lejano de la puerta
Y del chofer.

El sillón de cuero, mullido a fuerza de haber transportado
Miles de glúteos se adapta a mí y me trasmite la sensación de que
Estoy en el lugar adecuado, este es mi lugar en la vida y voy en la dirección
[correcta.

Pasamos las luces de comercios cerrados y de apartamentos con vida,
La gente se prepara para cenar o para irse a acostar.
Paso por esas escenas como si fueran de un mini teatro
Nomás para mí.

Veo gentes discutiendo, padres regañando
Adolescentes escapando de la generación paternal.
En algunas calles solo una que otra figura sigilosa camina
Como escondiendo un secreto, como huyendo con miedo.

El autobús se detiene y el viejo que se sentaba atrás de mi
Se baja con un pequeño veliz en la mano y el pesar de pasos lentos,
Muy pronto se convierte en otra sombra que es tragada por la oscuridad.

Como si nunca hubiera existido.

Aunque sé que nadie me espera
Me siento contento sabiendo que ya voy en mi camino.
El autobús hace otro alto para que baje una vieja
Que parecía dormida.

He tomado tantos autobuses a lo largo de mi vida,
Para ir a la escuela, para ir al trabajo, para visitar otras ciudades,
He viajado en autobuses de ranchos, de turistas, de obreros,
Pero esta vez es la primera que tomo el de la ruta setenta y seis.

Cuando las casas comienzan a escasear comienza un frío que se
Cuela por las destartaladas ventanas y se une la sensación de soledad.
El otro pasajero, un joven de apariencia obrera se apea de un brinco y
                    [se esfuma como humo de un cigarrillo apagado con prisa.

Por el espejo veo la cara del chofer y me doy cuenta de que
No es cansancio lo que desfigura su rostro, son facciones cadavéricas
                              [que lo hacen parecer la muerte.
Al darse cuenta de que lo miro voltea a verme, no puedo penetrar sus ojos.

Me asusto y con voz apagada le grito: "bajan."
Se voltea hacia el camino y con voz pastosa me responde:
"Ya no hay más paradas, hasta el final de la ruta."

MOJADO MONOLOGUE

Jesús Cortez

1990

HE LEFT, it's not like I didn't see it coming, pero ni modos... siquiera
me hubiera llevado con él...odio dormir en esta sala, todos nos miran
como bichos raros, dice mi mamá que el muerto y el arrimado a los
tres días apesta, and well I think she's right...and now my old man
leaves, but it's ok, we're in America now and life is supposed to be
better...dice mi brother que en unos días tendremos apartamento para
nosotros...espero que no tenga cucarachas como este... adiós
papá...mami, ¿¡tú no me vas a dejar verdad!? ¡Tú si me llevas contigo si
te vas!

1994

Damn!
My jefa says I should be careful
not be on the street so much
that they passed a fucken law
to try to get us to go back to Mexico.
She says they call it 187...like murder...
Chales...
And then she says they're putting more
migra at the border...I guess now I'll
never see my tía Cuca ever again...
Mom says to be good...
Guess she don't know how much I tried
to learn English quick, to lose my accent—
how I held back when called beaner,
wetback...and all the times I got my ass

kicked for trying to be "white" according
to my neighbors...
Forget this shit...I'm done with all of it...
I love you mama, but I gotta do what I gotta
do...and the streets keep showing me love...
and this fucken country keeps showing me hate!

1998

Graduation day...
damn...my mama never thought it would happen
why would she right? All those nights, and days
gone from the house, getting into shit...but it's here...
and I'm alone...my homies...gone...dead, jail...drop
outs...those who did alright have kids and a wife...I
miss them...but this diploma is for them too,
all the times they said "nah homie, stay in school, you're actually
smart"...and I guess I believed it...but now what?
I still aint got papers...college aint gonna happen...but at least
the fucken army stopped calling once I told them
I didn't have papers...damn...gotta sleep early after we celebrate
gotta start mowing lawns tomorrow...

2002

I was reading the paper today,
some law passed, ha, they say I can go to college now
aint that some shit...four years of reading and reading, trying to
maintain my sanity, trying to LEARN something...four years of
wondering if it was worth staying alive...wondering if it had
been better to die like the homies...this Marco Antonio
Firebaugh...I guess not all politicians are assholes after all...
now I gotta keep mowing lawns...gotta earn that money for school...
gotta get that degree...damn, but I'm old...fuck it, if my mama, and the
homies believe in me, I got this...damn! I'm actually excited...College,
here I come.

MOJADO IMMIGRANT BLUES

Jesús Cortez

THERE COMES a time for
mourning memories that
begin to fade into oblivion,
and you question if the smiles
and the tears even existed,

Sometimes it's hard to remember
the smell of rain, or the feeling
of muddy dirt streets on my feet—
I forget sometimes, until pain
reminds me of a town I have no love for,

Now that mama is gone,
I wonder if I'm telling the stories properly,
and if not, who do I ask for corrections?
I trust the spirits do not care about borders
and continue to guide me,

There is no love for me in amerika,
only the space we created,
with the same rejected people,
who found no place to belong at any time,
only got love for OUR Anaheim.

BURGUNDY DODGE ASPEN

Jesús Cortez

P ASKED IF I had a ranfla,
I replied "Simon, but it turns off"
when asked why I didn't drive
it to school—

There was joy in cruising
Beach blvd, on borrowed 12's,
bumping the Gap Band,
dodging police—

We used to wear hats,
someone told us it made foos
look older, hiding our bald
heads or short fades—

We cruised Magnolia Street,
until the Aspen went silent, and
the homies hid as they laughed
at what they called "the junk mobile"—

One night, I forgot about fear,
and drove down those Anaheim streets,
with a hurting face and pride,
searching for payback to ease the pain—

MISSING*

Michael Manerowski

THERE IS THE field
fenced in
where is the horse

there is the shoreline
waves endless
but no sails

there is the doorway
onto the street
the shadow
in the doorway

it is you now
missing

when will you step out
the sun is radiant

someone has got to find
the horse

someone has got to launch
the ships

*Originally published in *Laurel Review*.

AUSENTE

Michael Manerowski
Translated by Katherine Adcock

HE AHÍ EL campo
cercado
dónde está el caballo

he ahí la ribera
olas infinitas
mas velas ninguna

he ahí el portal
hacia la calle
la sombra
sobre el portal

ahora estás tú
ausente

cuando saldrás
el sol está radiante

alguien tiene que hallar
al caballo

alguien tiene que zarpar
los barcos

THERAPY FOR THE ALONE

Michael Manerowski

WHEN YOU ARRIVE
there will be sunlight
and loneliness
in the shadows
of the elm leaves

from your room window
you can see
into the courtyard
secretly
your pain

if on no one else
you can at least count
on the company
of your condition

when they can
a family member
or a distant friend may
drop you a line

between calls
to the silence
you may speak

as much as you like

no one will be there

with a tightness in their brow
to grow annoyed with the sound
of your voice

so speak if you will
recklessly
your weakness

even with loneliness
in the shadows
of the elm leaves

there is still a hope
for a therapy
in sunlight

TERAPIA PARA EL SOLITARIO

Michael Manerowski
Translated by Katherine Adcock

CUANDO LLEGUES
habrá luz de sol
y soledad
en las sombras
de las hojas de olmo

desde tu ventana
puedes ver
hacia el patio
en secreto
tu dolor

si con nadie más
al menos puedes contar
con la compañía
de tu condición

cuando puedan
un miembro familiar
o una amistad distante podría
comunicarse contigo

entre llamada y llamada
al silencio
podrías hablar

todo lo que quieras

nadie estará ahí
con el ceño fruncido
fastidiándose con el sonido
de tu voz

así que habla si quieres
sin cuidado
de tu debilidad

aun en soledad
en las sombras
de las hojas de olmo

aún hay esperanza
de una terapia
en la luz del sol

SHADOW OF THE HORSE

Michael Manerowski

IF ONLY I could see
through the dark
to the shadow

having lost the horse
having pulled up the fences
to the green gray meadow grasses
to the yellow wildflower
stars

having lost the freedom
lost the expanse
having lost the land
the sun the wind blowing
across the land

would not my hands be empty
of her rough and sweaty
velvet neck

would not my ears be empty
of her earth pounding
stone clomping
hooves

would not my heart
be empty
of the meadow
the sun the wind blowing

through the green gray grasses
blowing through the yellow wild
stars

the shadow of her neck
her cold black
wavy mane
galloping

through the freedom
through the meadow
through the sunlight
through my heart

SOMBRA DEL CABALLO

Michael Manerowski
Translated by Katherine Adcock

SI TAN SOLO pudiera ver
a través de la obscuridad
hacia la sombra

habiendo perdido el caballo
habiendo jalado las rejas
hacia los pastos de prado verde grisáceo
hacia las estrellas amarillas
de flor silvestre

habiendo perdido la libertad
perdido lo expandido
habiendo perdido la tierra
el sol el viento soplando
por toda la tierra

no estaría el vacío en mis manos
de su áspero y sudoroso
cuello de terciopelo

no estaría el vacío en mis oídos
de la tierra pulsante
las piedras sonantes
de sus pezuñas

no estaría el vacío
en mi corazón
del prado
el sol el viento soplando

por los pastos verde grisáceos
soplando por las salvajes
estrellas amarillas

la sombra de su cuello
su negro y frío
pelaje ondulado
galopando

atravesando la libertad
atravesando el campo
atravesando la luz del sol
atravesando mi corazón

IF LOVE IS AMOR

Jennifer Rathbun

–Un Beso Is Not a Kiss
Francisco X. Alarcón

IF A KISS is not un beso
I love you is not
te quiero ni mucho menos te amo
When you say te quiero
when you whisper it in my ear
do you really mean that
you love me
is there love
amor
because I make love with amor
y hago el amor con love
because if you really truly loved me
in one language or another
or in a wildly delicious unruly mix of the two
te quiero would never
ever be synonymous with adios
translated as goodbye

CORAZÓN TRANSVERSAL

Jennifer Rathbun

HIS HEART
su corazón
his heart beats sideways transversal
I want to give him mine
arrancármelo del pecho
still beating with my bare hands
his heart
su corazón
his heart beats sidewise transversal
and the world stands still
how long, how long
exijo respuesta
can a broken heart
beat
take mine
arrancármelo del pecho
with your bare hands
still beating
beating still
how long can his
heart beat sideways
transversal
norte al sur
it should beat north to south
como su herencia
Mexican
American
born on la frontera
in Arizona

his heart refused to
beat from north to south
beats transversal
side to side
instead
skipping along the border
instead of across it
side to side
like the rain
when it pours
and my tears
down my cheeks
side to side
me lo dijeron los doctores
I always knew his heart
su corazón
era diferente
take my heart
ahora
tear it out still beating
from my chest
north to south
norte al sur
chambers fill
currents flow
beat
beat
bea
be
e

A LA VIRGEN

Jennifer Rathbun

I PRAY TO la Virgen de Guadalupe
light her pink candle on my stove
rub silver pendant tucked under my shirt
make the sign of the cross
bare my sorrows and beg for
direction, a sign, some hope
a world with less lágrimas and
más amor, mucho más amor

It snows twelves inches
I'm shut in my home alone
snow comes in under my front
door and stains the hundred
year old hardwood floor black
frozen fingers rub over candle flames
but its wick is short and heat low

Virgencita protect me from the cold
bless me, bless my blue heart
bless this winter storm
my jewish sister says to light
an orange candle instead
but she doesn't tell me how to pray
what to say so I light an orange candle
under my crowned queen

Honeyed hues flicker off her
golden rays as whiteness
crystalizes the world outside and brings
everything to a standstill she tells
my heart to be still too and to know that she
is mi madre to trust in her
afterall if she can burn roses onto a tilma
that millions have adored across centuries
she can certainly renew my heart
in this winter storm

TRANSLATION

Jennifer Rathbun

I IMMERSE MYSELF in your language
intimately weave my tongue around yours
invite your poems to caress my hunger
stoke every pore of my being
as I light them on my lips
wet with your words
and recreate longings
do you ever wonder
what would it be like
to kiss in the flesh now
that I've translated
your every desire
and you've
penetrated
me in
verse

MEXICAN TIN HEARTS

Jennifer Rathbun

CROWNED AND WINGED
rubi red on sapphire blue

adorned with roses
or bearing the tree of life

collection of Mexican tin hearts
displayed on my walls

momentos from former loves
raised in Kansas

I watched the Wizard of Oz
as a young girl

time and time again
like the Tin Man I too

long for a
heart of flesh and blood

MANCINI'S

LR Cunningham

THE MINI-MART is still there,
        under New Management

Self-Checkout aisles
are tyrants of gravity,

I wore out my dignity,
bagging forgetful plastic
with spread oily fingers raised
I swear I didn't touch
Anything
or eat in the store.
        Scan the arrow, twice
Shoot.
        different masses as they fall to
Shit. unwanted items in the
Bagging, Area,
Needs Assistance, Needs Assistance
and I am seven again
caught crawling up the slide
with screech-handed shame
come to a halt
breathe easy, I remember;
to sip my Slurpee
with all supremacy.
with all due,
disrespect, remember, I am better
        than it.
that Methuselah donuts

are thrown out by eight

and age, after all, is overridden
and, if the night shift register shortens up,
we die, sugar,
donuts a Tan Volvo, rust crumbling
powder, rainbow sprinkles and a blue Rockstar
I corner the night and she is mine

EL PRIDE

LR Cunningham

ENTRE LOS DOS seguiríamos llegando
a los mismos bares que siempre, de los cincuenta
Queers con pulsos en la península.
cruzamos la calle a toda y obvia
velocidad olímpica,
esquivándonos y encontrándonos
es decir;
me gusta cómo me hieres
pero no tanto,
como el gato de mi ex, no, ese,
el otro, que
rasguñaba siempre competitivamente
ése mismo suéter, tu favorito que compramos
en Santa Cruz jugando a ser turistas,
en la casa que dejamos
con memorias gruesas
Suavemente: BÉ SA ME.
Gritan unos homos en la playa
Durante la estación de los Géminis
me devuelves las llamadas.
nací en la luna, negra, hondamente moribunda,
vos en las estrellas
con complejo de dios, confeccionando personalidades múltiples
y ya empezamos
con nuestras mariconadas
Para el Pride 2018, fuimos a ver a una Reina,
al Drag más mediocre del mundo.
compartimos la sensación aguda
de perder el ritmo

uno apenas bailable
de buscar entre la mierda y las entradas pagadas
mirándonos y luego al suelo
a las pestañas falsas apretadas como cochinillas
una razón para quedarnos
juntos

MONOGAMÍAS

LR Cunningham

ENTRÉ SOLA A la exhibición de Óptica;
espectáculos cosmológicos, decían
haciendo cola con seis pies de espacio
para todos
El docente del museo les dice que miren hacia abajo
salvo a mí, la monógama del Arte Moderno, siendo freak
si se marean, shiny happy tourists, dice, entonces,
no oigo más
llego y espero
sentirme bien, macabra.
enfermarme del estómago
no me parece mucho
pedir, suspiro
Y me interrumpe, ya tuvo su turno,
señora,
me envejece
El tiempo no permitirá más

THE INTIMACY OF
ALTERNATIVE UNIVERSES

Lisandra Pérez

BETWEEN ERECT PINTO beans
is your mole   is
the inside of your home
mothering the hair on your legs
yes   you can
here   & you will
inside this mole is the curl
on the corner of your lips
soft skin burns sand
paper   like
          somewhere in Michoacán

we flatten masa with our hands, el comal
Michoacán sun, rough blistered fingers
a stranger calls your name, a relative
sings about frogs, *así te sanas* dice
fantasize all the possibilities of living
find the moss lined mountains awake
is the body you condemn, a world
you furnished to feel like home— right now
bloated church-ladies unravel their fans

SLEEP: THE B-SIDE

Lisandra Pérez

TWO PARTNERS AGO, I learned to chew my English
before the decorum lost its charisma & now
my tongue has made peace with the phlegm
it houses. Near the Chattanooga River, I
almost drove us off the cliff-side, I forget why
we fought in the first place. Tongues unknowing
me dijo que estaba embarazado. That he's pregnant
or embarrassed of my clothes. I always dream
we fall off. That our bodies are helium-filled
& we float back to the cliffs, above the tumbling
car until the distance makes the river run calm—
nuestro metal y sus peleas una orquesta de olas.
No te digo que al fin respiro. En vez te susurro in our dream
tongue about the silliness of it all, how Earth
is truly green and blue from up here.

IN YOUR SLEEP THERE'S A ROAD
THAT TAKES US TO ZACATECAS

Lisandra Pérez

WE'VE NEVER been, but a donkey waits for us at your door. We wear our finest clothes and fold your mattress until it fits in our front pocket. The road is south bound— it's nothing special, but it's all we have so we go. We sweat our way through copper fields more rusted than golden and Iowa disintegrates as quickly as our shoes, so we get rid of them. Este sueño es mudo, pero aún preguntó ¿Has oído a mi cuerpo dudar de la colina? ¿Llorar a la luna? ¿Preguntar si crees que alguien nos espera? Our mothers come in threes, entre rebozos de manta. Se aflijan la pérdida como si ya hubiera pasado. Un poco como tú. When we get to the border, our feet are raw from dancing around leather rosaries you never learned to use, letters from mothers begging for our return, and clothes I don't remember packing. We suck the marrow off the bone— I can't tell if it's animal or human, but right now the horizon is a line in your eyes and I know you've made it home.

LION TAMER

Colin Ian Jeffery

GREAT LIONEL WAS a lion tamer, intrepid, bold and true
Star of the circus, daredevil of the sawdust ring
Bravery second to none, a hero knowing no fear.
Introduced by the ringmaster he steps in the ring
Wearing red satin tights, purple vest, and black boots
Cracking his whip with pistol on hip, so haughty and proud
Fearlessly enters the lions cage with contemptuous grin
Confronting three elderly lions and bad-tempered lioness.
The audience cheer and Great Lionel bows and waves,
Cracking his whip, the three lions obey leaping on barrels
Quiet and still, ready to perform and follow his commands.
But lioness refuses, sullen and hungry, wanting her dinner
She ate Great Lionel leaving only whip and black leather boots.

EAGLE AND THE HARE

Colin Ian Jeffery

GOLDEN EAGLE FLOATS upon the wind
Above a Scottish Glen, eyes searching
Swaying heather far below seeking prey.

Nervous hare, nose twitching, ever fearful
Standing on hind legs looking for danger
Not seeing death high above upon the wing
And feeling safe returns to eating grass.

The eagle folds wings and drops to kill
Silent and deadly, talons open to grab
Hare terrified as talons dig into fur and flesh
Screams and is snatched away to be eaten.

VOICES

Colin Ian Jeffery

VOICES FROM LONG ago call echoing in my dreams
Memories of childhood, joyous, sweet, and innocent
Bright golden summers that seemed never-ending
When happiness reigned supreme with days rich with love
Family supporting and encouraging, guiding my way.
Now, my parents and brother are long gone and grave deep
And I am burdened with old age, anthric bones, blood pressure
Alone, difficulty walking with time cruelly speeded up,
Destination the grave and final sleep coming ever closer.
Throughout life I sought for meaning and truth
Finding the blue planet was like a single grain of sand
Lost among vast desert of stars expanding ever outwards
Away into an eternal blackness of space with limit unknown,
While wondering on the existence of a loving God.

TODAS LAS CIUDADES VIVIERON
EN MIS OJOS

Jorge Manzanilla Pérez

I

MI MADRE CRECIÓ entre las huellas de un pantano. De la pólvora.
Su memoria aun recorre los rostros de caudillos que disparan a
                                        [quemarropa
Su memoria aún recorre los caudillos que disparan la nostalgia
y se atreven a mirar nuestro presente.
Hablan con la boca llena de odio
y nunca tragan los nombres de la guerra.
Así mi abuela toma el aserrín de las enaguas
prepara las tortillas que bordan silencio.
El fuego destila su luz y regresa a mi madre
como los muertos regresan a donde se supieron vivos.
Porque toda ciudad dibuja cada uno de sus sueños
porque toda ciudad habla de sus muertos
antes que de sus vivos.
Por eso mi padre nos bautiza desde la ceniza de noviembre
hasta el rosal de una primavera ausente.
Si se habla de guerra, hay que abrir las entrañas de la calle.
Olvidar el desnudo de la infancia.
porque esta es la memoria de nuestro polvo.

II

No conocí las ciudades que pasaron por mi casa.
Dibujé mi infancia con la garganta abierta,

sin las entrañas del eco.
No sólo se habló de nuestros primos caídos

Allá afuera está la guerra, tu padre no aparece.

Gritó el abandono y calló mi madre.
Mi encierro penetra los cinco años.
Afuera las balas abren su cauce
y así iniciamos el catecismo.

III

Los milagros nacen vacíos
y todos callan.
El otoño crece y deshoja los pájaros.
En este cuerpo hay parques, escuelas
y otra ciudad entre los labios.
Nadie se atreve a pronunciar
porque hace falta un rayo
que venga y no se vaya
porque sólo así nos iluminamos.
Tenemos un sol que sale de los dientes
Así nos tragamos las palabras y las mañanas.

IV

Dios entra a la tumba de mi padre y divide el camposanto en la
[fracción del pan.
El aire cercena la lumbre mientras mis primos tejen su espanto.
Mi madre abraza el verbo que no se ha hecho carne
y mi abuela nos cubre la herida de nostalgia.
La hiel abre sus piernas y bebo del sexo muerto.
Me duele la espalda de tanta ciudad que cargo
Yo no tengo las palabras que puedan vestirme.

Yo no tengo un río de hojas.

[Acá nada fluye]

Esto no sé si es un sueño o el tizne de un delirio.
No sé quién está cortando el vuelo a los pájaros.

[Acá nada fluye]

Quiero dejar a mis muertos y se me caen los espejos de los ojos.
Entonces ¿para qué nos subimos al altar que no nos corresponde?
No sé cuántas guerras habitan la ciudad.
Yo no me conformo con beberme los pueblos y darlos de ofrenda.
Ojalá que todo no fuera tan frágil.

BALERO

Jorge Manzanilla Pérez

A MI PAPÁ lo vieron robarse treinta años
y nunca quiso devolverlos. Todo engaño
es un castigo, en sus ojos comenzó a
regar la lluvia y así perpetuó su infancia.
Mi papá se robó los columpios de los parques,
robó todo libro que hablara sobre el padre,
recortó treinta años y los pegó a su nuevo balero de madera.
En abril del 50 se enfermó por tragarse
malas palabras. En mayo rompió el cielo
y en junio arrancó el viento de árboles
para dibujarlos en un lugar común.

Él era un niño y yo su diente de leche.

Ahora digo papá y se cierra la ventana.
Estoy de espaldas al dolor del fuego,
el agua del duelo me sabe a soledad,
agua que pudre en el nombre de Dios.

El mar se levanta hacia adentro de los párpados,
Cierre los ojos, inhale y retenga:
¿A quién no le ha dolido el tiempo?
Esas palabras que piensa están corriendo por la sangre.

Espere.

Esto que siente es una serpiente muda que viene del pecho.
Ahora exhale y diga su nombre.
Repita y verá esa fotografía
en la alcoba de sus arterias.
Eso que siente es un recuerdo
y tiene tonalidades en grises.
Yo sé a lo que se refiere
cuando expresa: "Se me está cerrando el cielo".
Dios se nos muere de vez en cuando
y aceptamos el luto de estar solos.
Las almas se desprenden de sus hojas
porque están cansadas de morir tantas veces.
Yo me refiero a papá
        cuando se dibuja el rostro del siempre ausente,
        el siempre cuerpo sin espejo,
        la misma mirada de vitral sin fondo,
        la sed del día en plena rabia.
En la mano derecha mi puño traga el pulso de la hiel
En la mano izquierda, el milagro nunca sucede.

Sucederá el incendio, que de eso comemos,
Seremos píldora, seremos tumba
porque de esto estamos acostumbrados.

Papá usó crayones para dibujar la infancia. Lo que usted no sabe,
    es que está dibujando este poema, luego dibujará la memoria.
Recordemos que en mi herida hay un pueblo muriendo de hambre.

EL DOLOR ES UN ANIMAL QUE HA MUERTO EN MI PECHO

Jorge Manzanilla Pérez

LA VOZ DE mi padre me destierra del eco y de su sombra.
la voz de mi padre aún opaca los espejos,
la voz de mi padre abre la mañana y baja el telón de la noche,
la voz de mi padre repite el cruce de Juárez – El Paso
porque le sobra el tiempo y no se cansa de repetir su muerte.
La voz de mi padre juega con el silencio de mi cuerpo
y me voy sumiendo lentamente hacia dentro.
Tengo un pecho dentro de otro pecho
y una voz que descifra otra voz
que es precisamente, la de mi padre.

I

Repito tantas veces "mi padre" para invocar lo invisible. Sé que en alguna repetición atravesará el Puente Norte y logrará la hazaña por la que perdió la vida. Una hazaña solar que todo inmigrante necesita. Repito tantas veces "mi padre, mi padre, mi padre", porque al nombrar una luz emerge entre Juárez y El Paso y forja palabras, que en algún momento, serán pronunciadas. Hable con sus hijos de noche, porque no sabemos cuántas veces veremos el amanecer en sus ojos. Repita el nombre de sus muertos y ponga una veladora y una Santa Muerte que acobije su Última Cena. Ponga un altar, porque en la Frontera, todos los días se celebra a los Santos Muertos y a los Santos Inocentes. Todo inmigrante es un pan de muerto que espera ser devorado por alguna constitución. Todo inmigrante morirá en el estómago de las patrullas fronterizas. Repita el nombre de sus muertos, no se canse, agote su voz, agote sus ojos. Quiero que usted tome esta página conmigo y evoque la oración por la que estamos reunidos. No pare. Estamos pronunciando al mismo tiempo nuestros muertos. Se aclara la página y su mente está proyectando los ojos de sus parientes caídos por un Sueño Americano. Yo ya tomé la veladora y trago la bilis y la angustia de un narrador invisible que ora atrás de mi oreja. Usted se cansa como yo y tira los brazos al suelo porque estamos huérfanos. Agarre su repetición y no apague la veladora, porque esto es la ausencia de un cuerpo.

II

Esta Santa Muerte pide por el cruce y por la ceguera de la patrulla fronteriza. Vea su destino, mire a la familia que lo espera del otro lado. No hay malla, no hay muro, tampoco está su cuerpo. Su cuerpo está velando a mis muertos. Su cuerpo está orando para evocar a los caídos. Este altar abre los puntos cardinales y ora con mirra. Son las tres de la mañana, son las tres de la mañana. Su cuerpo es un templo y yo soy su misa. Su cuerpo está en derrumbe y voy entrando por el ojo de su mano y por el cruce de El Paso – Juárez. Aquí está su padre, aquí está su noche.

La mesa está puesta.

FICCIÓN

ESCRIBIR PARA EXISTIR

¿Para qué sirve la literatura? Muchas y extrañas son las posibles respuestas. Preguntas de idiosincrática interpretación y exasperante complejidad. ¿Por qué leemos literatura? La búsqueda de algo que solo se encuentra en la experiencia lectora de una especificidad temporal y espacial, propia o ajena. Leemos, aquí y ahora pero la misma lectura en el pasado o en el futuro arroja diferentes resultados y por ello seguimos leyendo hasta no leer más, como la vida misma.

¿Para qué se escribe literatura? Tal vez, una de esas complejas e inalcanzables respuestas a la pregunta de por qué literatura, sea la absorción de una experiencia de otro. Ya sea otra persona diferente o seamos nosotros o sea otro nosotros diferente como persona al que fuimos en el pasado, al que somos ahora, o al que seremos en el futuro. Acaso sea una necesidad de comunicarse o de comunicar algo. Quizás sea simplemente ser.

En los cuentos de este volumen se comunica la intransitividad de una existencia singular. En "Vidas escondidas" de **Andrea Zelaya** se nos presenta una confesión de futuro híbrido no por apocalíptico menos esperanzador; en "The Movies" de **Theo Czajkowski** experimentamos el gozo del personaje que se sabe estando en el lugar adecuado en un momento suspendido en el tiempo, casi como un hechizo de película; en "Latchkey Girl" de **Jonathan Ferrini**, nos retrotraemos a la niñez ajena y la satisfacción propia de que la resolución de nuestros problemas vitales sean matemáticamente satisfactorios; finalmente en "A Creature of Hurt and Memory and Intention" de **Michael McGuire** se nos retrata un momento minúsculo en la vida de dos donnadies pero que muestra la densidad de una existencia entera.

En resumen, es el ansia de sentir y comunicar lo que vertebra estos cuentos que esperamos que ustedes, queridos lectores, disfruten tanto como lo hemos hecho los editores durante su selección.

LATCHKEY GIRL

Jonathan Ferrini

"TEACHER, ANNA IS pretending to sleep again!"

"Anna, pay attention to my lecture!

"You dare ignore me!

"I'm marching you down to the principal right now.

"Read your textbooks students until I return!"

"Mrs. Diaz, Anna's teacher removed her from class. She's remained unresponsive to me.

"Anna has learning difficulties. In geometry class, she placed her head on the desk between her arms and ignored her teacher.

"She's bullied because her clothing with cartoon caricatures is age inappropriate for a teenager.

"Anna is seventeen and there isn't anything more we can teach her. I have no choice but to expel her from school.

"You might take her to the armed forces recruiting office who may enlist her. She might earn a GED. Ask for 'Sergeant Diaz' who may help her pass the aptitude tests."

"Senora Principal, I want Anna to have a better life than me. I sew clothes by day and clean offices by night. I'm a single mother. Anna never knew her father. Anna has a big heart but didn't receive the gifts of beauty or smarts. I fear she'll never leave our crime ridden, poor neighborhood in the South Bronx."

"Good luck to both of you Mrs. Diaz."

They call me a "special ed" student because I can't read well. The words appear jumbled to me. My teachers never inquired about my reading disability. I was too embarrassed to say anything.

I learn easily with pictures.

I liked Geometry class because the teacher used different color chalk to draw the triangles, squares, and circles. I knew the teacher was seeking the answer to the area of an Isosceles triangle she drew in pink, green, and blue chalk. I visualized "Heron's Formula" from the textbook picture and calculated the answer in seconds.

I buried my face within my arms and pretended to be sleeping because being bullied for being smart is worse than being bullied for being a "special ed" student.

I'm bored watching television and sitting on the stoop all day waiting for Mama to come home from sewing clothes in a "sweat shop". She warned me not venture off the stoop, fearing the crime and drugs of the neighborhood lined with boarded up stores, abandoned cars, and trash.

I looked forward to our mail carrier, Mrs. Washington's arrival.

"Hello, Anna. How you doing today?

"I heard they don't want you in school anymore, darling."

"Yeah, I miss school but it doesn't miss me. Any mail for us today?"

"Just advertisements.

"Let me tell you a secret I've learned delivering the mail for thirty years. Some folks receive good mail and most people receive bad mail, but, sooner or later, good mail arrives in everybody's mailbox, even yours!

"Someday good mail will come to you. I hope I deliver it to you, honey.

"I'll see you tomorrow, Anna."

Mama gave me $5 every day to cross the street to "Dreamz Burger". I enjoy their juicy burgers, fries, and a strawberry shake. The owner, Mr. Morales, is a nice man.

Although I was hungry, I didn't want to spend Mama's hard-earned money and would return it to her when she arrived home with groceries. We looked forward to enjoying a homecooked meal together before Mama rushed off to her evening janitorial job on Wall Street, a long subway ride from the South Bronx.

"Hey 'Zombie' girl! Why do you dress like a kid in those ankle high sneakers, overalls, and cartoon shirt? You got kicked out of school because you crazy!"

"I might have been 'kicked out of school' but I didn't drop out like you jerks."

"Come off that stoop. I'll buy you some lipstick and be your 'special ed teacher'."

"Come on Jorge, let her be, man!"

"Don't forget whose boss, Alberto!"

Our neighborhood gang is named the "Los Muertos". Alberto is a new recruit. I don't think he's a bad boy like the rest of them. He has a kind face and is cute. As they continued down the sidewalk, Alberto turned and smiled at me.

One hot, muggy afternoon, I saw an elderly man struggling to carry an old movie projector along the sidewalk. He stopped several times to catch his breath and cough. I was concerned about his safety. Even though Mama warned me never to leave the safety of the stoop, I ran across the street, dodging honking cars, to offer assistance to the old man.

"I'm Alma. Can I help you, Sir"?

"No necessito assistancia, Chica".

The old man took a deep breath, and resumed carrying the heavy projector to the door of the long since shuttered "El Viaje" movie theatre. He carefully placed the projector on the sidewalk while reaching into his pocket for a key which opened an alley door into the theatre. I noticed a steep set of stairs leading up to an apartment. He picked up the heavy projector, and, as he attempted to climb the stairs, fell backwards. I immediately steadied him.

"Sir, please let me help you."

"Gracias, Chica. You lift from one end, and I the other."

We reached the top of the stairs and door to the apartment. The old man had a persistent cough. He opened the door, and we carried the projector into an unkempt apartment above the movie theatre. The walls were adorned with vintage movie posters and the apartment was stacked with metal film cannisters from floor to ceiling. Piles of books about cinema were strewn about the apartment. A movie projector was sitting atop a podium and pointed towards a white wall serving as a screen.

"Gracias, Chica. I have no money to pay you."

"My name isn't 'Chica'. It's Alma. Even though we're both Puerto Rican, I don't speak Spanish.

"I apologize, Alma. I'm Domingo."

"What's all this stuff you have in here?"

"I rescued this old 'Simplex' 35mm projector from a closing theatre.

"I started as an usher at this theatre at sixteen. I was promoted to projectionist which earned me a union card, and a small pension. I rent the 'El Viaje' from the Bloom family. Let me show you around".

I noticed a meager kitchen consisting of instant coffee, Ramen noodles, canned ravioli, chili, and saltine crackers with only a hot plate. A small cot was the only furniture above which he tacked the original movie poster from the 1958 movie "Around the World in 80 days" co-starring famed Mexican comedic actor, "Cantinflas".

He ran to the sink and coughed up blood.

"You're sick Domingo. What's hurting you?"

"I have lung cancer.

"I'll show you the projection room."

We entered a room with two large metal projectors, each having a top and bottom reel the size of hubcaps with a lens pointed out rectangular cut-aways in the wall.

"Look through those windows and you can see the theatre below. It's dark now because I can't afford to put on the electricity.

"Let me teach you to thread the film through the projector. It took me a better part of a year to learn it so don't get frustrated."

He turned on a switch, and the reels began to turn on each projector.

"Each of these two reels hold about two thousand feet of film and require six to eight changes during a film. The upper reel is the 'feed' reel and the lower is the 'take up reel'."

"Why do you need to run two projectors?"

"After the first reel runs about eighteen minutes, two dots will appear on the screen, alerting me to begin the second projector which will commence where the other projector left off without the audience ever knowing."

I watched Domingo thread the film which caught the sprocket

and quickly began to wind through the projector like a rollercoaster ride. Suddenly, movie credits for "Snow White" appeared on the giant screen below.

"You try, Alma."

The reels were heavy. I secured both the "feed reel" and "take up" reel. I opened the hatch to the side of the projector to thread the film which caught the sprockets. The film left my fingers darting towards the lens at "24 frames per second" according to Domingo.

"Anna, you're a natural."

"But how does the audience see and hear the film, Domingo?"

"It's the 'gate' and 'shutter'. The gate holds the film still while the shutter is open. The shutter interrupts the emitted light during the time the film is advanced to the next frame. The audience doesn't see the transition which tricks their brains into believing a moving image is on screen.

"Look at the film stock including two-channel audio signals recorded as a pair of lines which creates the sound.

"One day, we disassemble the broken "Simplex" projector, examine all the parts, and I'll let you put it back together. Let me show you how to splice film".

Domingo placed white cotton gloves onto my hands. He held my hands and was patient, slow, and deliberate in placing the two exact frames of film atop each other onto a metal film splicer. He lowered the lever with the blade down onto the film, splicing it, and applied a clear cement to bind the two ends of film together.

Domingo's cough was becoming more intense.

"May I bring you some cough medicine, Domingo?"

"I'm tired and need to sleep."

"May I come again, Domingo?"

"Why aren't you in school?"

"The school doesn't think I'm smart enough and kicked me out."

"Not smart enough?

'Putos'.

"It took me a year to learn to become a projectionist.

"You come back tomorrow and I show you more."

"May I read the Simplex projector manual tonight. I'll bring it back tomorrow."

"Sure, take the manual but know it's the original operator's manual and irreplaceable. Lock the door behind you, Alma."

After returning home, I studied each image of the projection manual. I closed my eyes after each image, and could clearly see the details of the illustration showing all the parts. The operation of the projector was committed to my memory.

The following evening, after Mama left for her evening janitor job, I took a plate of left overs to Domingo. Domingo spliced together yards of "Traveltalks", short films from the 1930's about faraway places played just before the movie began. He had me thread the film through his projector on the podium, and we watched the wonders of the world projected against his barren old wall.

"Anna, make certain you see the world!

"These short movies take me to places I'll never see. You still have the opportunity."

"I read the "Simplex" operators manual last night, Domingo. Would you allow me to disassemble it, repair, and reassemble it?"

"You kidding me, Alma?"

"I know everything about the projector, Domingo."

"Let's see what you learned. Use these tools."

I quickly disassembled the old projector, tightened a loose sprocket, and reassembled the projector like an easy jigsaw puzzle.

"I fixed it, Domingo."

"You have a talent, Alma. This working vintage projector is now worth good money! You can make a career repairing projectors if you choose!

"How did you learn to do this overnight?"

"I memorized the illustration within the owner's manual showing me the workings of the projector."

"Your school did you a favor. With your talents, you'll be making more money than the principal!"

So began my relationship with Domingo; eating dinner together, watching films, and talking movie history.

One evening, I decided to treat Domingo to a Dreamz Burger. I clutched the five-dollar bill in my hand and ordered the usual, hamburger, fires, and strawberry shake.

Los Muertos entered the store, and just as I was ready to pay, the leader, Jorge, grabbed the five-dollar bill from my hand saying,

"That's mine, now, Zombie girl!"

The gang laughed but was interrupted by the store manager, Mr. Morales, shouting,

"Get out of my store you punks and don't come back!"

"Let's get out of this dump!

"Hey customers, there's rats in this joint!"

Alberto was the last to exit, and he reached into his pocket, handing me a $5 bill. Our eyes met, and we shared a smile.

"Take this bottle of cerveza to Domingo and say it's from his old friend, Morales at Dreamz Burger. No charge for anything."

After eating, I asked Domingo if I could make an attempt to organize his collection of films, posters, and books.

"Go at it, Alma. I've long forgotten what I have. I've been collecting films and equipment from closing theatres all over town for decades."

I learned about film by organizing Domingo's collection according to film styles depicted in one of his cinema textbooks.

As I delved further into Domingo's collection of cinema books, I saw beautiful images of many different types of films including,

Hollywood, German, French, Italian, Japanese, Korean, Mexican, silents, and many more.

I dreamed the El Viaje could share these films from throughout the world with the neighborhood.

Movies showed me a world beyond the South Bronx. The thought provoking images, themes, acting, lighting, locations, and directing brought me happiness. I wanted to share this with Mama, but working day and night, she wouldn't have the time.

After months of organizing Domingo's film collection, he approached me with an announcement,

"I have a special surprise for you.

"We're watching a movie the way movies are meant to be

enjoyed."

Domingo reached for a switch, and the lights of the spectacular old theatre flickered to life revealing an ornate ceiling, red plush seats, and a balcony.

"I chose a special movie for you Anna to express my gratitude for all of your hard work."

We spent Saturday afternoon sitting in the dark theatre, hearing the pitter patter of rats running about, eating popcorn, drinking soda, and watching one of my favorite films, the original 1950 Disney classic, "Cinderella". Domingo allowed me to change the reels throughout the film.

The months passed quickly spending time with Domingo.

It was Halloween night. Domingo planned an evening of selected horror films beginning with the famous silent, "Nosferatu." I brought Dreamz Burgers, fries, soda, and a beer for Domingo.

When I knocked, I heard no answer. Domingo gave me a key for entry in case of emergency. I unlocked the door, ran up the stairway, and found him sweating and shivering under the blanket in his cot. I noticed bloody paper napkins he coughed into strewn about the floor.

"Domingo, what is wrong with you?"

"It's my time to pass."

"I'm calling 911!"

"No!

"I have no phone and won't die in a hospital charity ward!"

"Mama won't let me have a cell phone. I'll run to Dreamz Burger and call 911."

Domingo began to cry,

"No!

"Let me die amongst these films I love!"

Just at that moment, we heard the back door to the theatre being pried open. The theatre was pitch dark.

Los Muertos entered with the goal of stealing anything valuable, and setting fire to the theatre which they were suspected of doing throughout the neighborhood. The nitrate film stock collected by Domingo would burn down the entire block.

"It's Los Muertos, Domingo. What do we do?"

He raised his feeble, shaking arm, pointing towards a stack of metal film cans.

"Pick the one titled, 'Don't Break the Law Children'. Thread it and keep the lights off in the auditorium."

I hurried as the Los Muertos crept about. Alberto muttered,

"Let's get out of this creepy place."

I watched the black and white film thread through the projector. Suddenly, sounds of iron doors rolling shut and locking filled the pitch-dark theatre.

A frightened man screams,

"Please release me from this hell!"

I viewed a filthy prison cell with a body lying in the corner covered in blood, and prisoners kicking the helpless victim.

Los Muertos watched the screen with horrified expressions.

A gruesome image showed a man strapped to a chair in a gas chamber suffocating from the poisonous gas as he pleaded for mercy,

"Please, let me live!"

The screen went black but the sound track warned,

"Break the law and you might also die in prison. We're waiting for you boys and girls!"

Domingo pointed to an empty, glass soda bottle, and mumbled,

"Roll this down the aisle, now!"

I quietly opened the door to the projection room, crawled to the aisle, and rolled the glass soda bottle down the concrete sloped floor making a startling clanking noise.

"Hey, man, what's that rolling down the aisle?"

The rats who lived comfortably within the theatre didn't appreciate the intrusion and crawled over the gang seeking escape out the open door.

"Damn, a rat just crawled up my leg. Let's get out of here!"

The horrifying film and rats frightened Los Muertos who ran for the exit door.

I returned to the projection room and peered out the tiny glass window and saw only Alberto remaining, looking up at me with a smile.

I turned to Domingo who was unusually still with a happy grin on his face.

"Domingo, they're gone!"

He didn't respond. I laid my fingers upon his wrists and felt no pulse, then placed my face against his mouth. There was no breath. He had passed.

I gently placed the blanket over his head and a reel of film within his arms. I pulled the switch lighting up the beautiful theatre. Even the rats were silent in memory of their fallen friend.

I joined Alberto who accompanied me to Dreamz Burger where we explained the situation to Mr. Morales who called 911.

I missed Domingo.

Mama was worrying about my future, and I realized I'd have to take a job soon. Mama joined me on the stoop, handing me a soda pop.

"What are you going to do for work?

"I won't have you sewing and scrubbing floors like me.

"I'm taking you down to see Sergeant Diaz at the recruiting station. He'll get you enlisted in the service, and maybe they train you to type, and when you leave military, you get a job with one of the Wall Street "big shots" whose office I clean?"

"Hey, Mama. Mrs. Washington has mail for us."

"Special letter addressed to Alma marked 'Return Receipt Required'.

"Please sign here, Alma."

I couldn't read very well and English wasn't Mama's first language, so I asked Mrs. Washington to open it and read it aloud.

"I'll read it. These big shot law firms don't scare this old mail carrier!

"The letter is from a lawyer representing the estate of Domingo inviting you to a meeting regarding the will and asking you to call to make an appointment."

"My English not good, Mrs. Washington. Please make an appointment for me and Alma."

Mrs. Washington dialed, and began speaking,

"I'm calling on behalf of Ms. Alma Diaz and her mother who received communication from your office regarding the last will and testament of Domingo Sanchez. They wish to make an appointment."

"I start my janitorial work on Wall Street at seven. Alma can meet me at their Wall Street office at 5:30 pm."

"Alma Diaz and her mother can arrange to meet at 5:30 any weekday."

"Thursday at 5:30 pm. Confirmed."

Mrs. Washington knelt down and hugged me, whispering,

"I told you 'Good mail' would come to you. I'm blessed to have delivered it to you."

Mama and I entered the attorney's office on the top floor of a high-rise office building. The heavy walnut doors opened, revealing a commanding view of New York. The thick red carpeting was like walking on a cloud. We were immediately greeted by the receptionist.

"Hello, Mrs. Diaz and Alma. The attorney and Mrs. Bloom are waiting in the conference room."

She opened the door revealing a large conference table surrounded by green leather upholstered chairs. The walls were covered in beautiful paneling with framed oil paintings of important people.

The attorney and an elegantly dressed woman my mother's age both stood and approached.

"Hello Mrs. Diaz and Anna. I'm Heidi Bloom, the Executor of the estate. This is my attorney, Elliott Gold. It's our pleasure to meet you ladies."

I was transfixed by the beautiful diamonds on Mrs. Blooms fingers and neckline which drew me into them like a movie screen recalling scenes from many of the movies I watched with Domingo:

"Toto, I've got a feeling we're not in Kansas anymore."

"Here's looking at you, kid."

"May the Force be with you."

"I'm Charles Foster Kane."

Each of the diamonds within her tennis bracelet shined like a movie marque.

"I'm the attorney representing the estate of Mr. Domingo Sanchez and his Executor, Mrs. Bloom who was his landlord and employer for many years."

"Elliott, please allow me to take it from here."

"Of course, Mrs. Bloom."

"My grandparents loved Domingo like a son and taught him to become the projectionist of the El Viaje.

"My parents and myself chose corporate careers and weren't interested in operating the theatre. Once my grandparents died, El Viaje fell into disrepair and closed. I maintained Domingo as a caretaker to watch over the theatre which hasn't shown a film for over a decade.

"I inherited the property and have considered selling it. None of the interested buyers are movie theatres; mostly condo developers and tech retail giants who will change the neighborhood, they say, "for the good." My grandparents loved your neighborhood and knew many of its neighbors by name. It would break their hearts to see your neighborhood become gentrified and overpriced.

"Domingo willed you a life insurance policy from the projectionist's union which will get you started, and, along with 'sweat equity', you can complete a substantial rehab of the El Viaje, if you choose. Alternatively, you may take the insurance money, the films, posters, and books he willed to you. I suspect many of these possessions are valuable.

"However, if you choose to open the theatre, I'll rent it to you for $1 per month for 12 months."

Mrs. Bloom began to weep.

"Look at this old photo, Alma. You look remarkably like my grandmother when she opened the theatre with my grandfather. She ran the ticket booth, concession stand, and grandfather operated the projection equipment until Domingo came aboard."

It was an old black and white photo of two young people standing in front of the theatre as the neon "El Viaje" sign was being installed above the marque. They were happy and in love. I saw Mama wiping a tear from her eye.

"After the first year of successfully operating the theatre, I'll sell the building to you with no down payment, and carry the loan at a very reasonable mortgage payment so you afford to stay in business.

"Domingo told me how you organized the priceless nitrate films which are disintegrating, the movie posters, books, and projection equipment. He told me you had a 'photographic memory' for images, and are a 'wiz' with projection equipment.

"If you choose not to open El Viaje, in addition to the insurance proceeds, I can arrange an auction of the films, posters, projectors, and books if you would like the proceeds, or, you might consider 'paying forward' and donating them to a film preservation society."

"Excuse me. May I speak with my daughter alone for a moment."

"Certainly, Mrs. Diaz. Mr. Gold and myself will step out of the room while you speak."

The heavy walnut doors closed, and Mama spoke.

"You're a teenage girl. Do you believe you can open that old theatre again?"

"I'm very good at operating projectors and editing film."

"Where did you learn this, Alma?"

"My friend, Domingo.

"I need you to help me with the ticket booth, concession stand, and maintenance. It will be our business, Mama! You can quit your two jobs. I'll need you full-time."

"What if you fail? I don't think you find a good job in movie theatres today?"

"I won't fail and Mrs. Bloom will sell El Viaje to me when I make it a success. I have so many special films the neighborhood will pay to see. We'll live comfortably. We can fix up Domingo's apartment above the theatre and live rent free.

"I need your help, mama, please! It's the only passion I have."

Mama held me tight, whispering,

"I'll work my fingers to the bone to make the theatre a success, Alma."

As we began renovation of El Viaje, Mr. Morales paid for a "Coming Soon" banner which was hung over the marque. Many neighbors offered donations and skilled tradesmen donated work.

The disbanded "Los Muertos" gang boys, missing Jorge who was jailed, donated their time, learning building trades from the skilled workers.

Mrs. Bloom provided legal and accounting services for the many contracts we were required to sign with vendors and movie distributors.

In ninety days of around the clock work, the El Viaje marque was glowing, and a line formed around the block to watch our opening premier of the documentary film, "Rita Moreno: Just A Girl Who Decided To Go For It".

Mama worked the ticket booth, recently retired Mrs. Washington ran the concession stand, and Alberto, so handsome in his red uniform with gold epaulets, greeted each of the guests as our usher.

I hung a copy of Mrs. Bloom's grandparents' photo within the lobby along with the original movie poster of Domingo's beloved film,

"Around the World In 80 Days."

It was the only poster I retained, "paying forward" Domingo's possessions to film preservation societies, film schools, and libraries who "paid it back" by selecting El Viaje for prestigious film festivals and the premier of independent films selected for international award recognition.

New restaurants, markets, and curio stores opened, revitalizing the neighborhood.

School taught me to calculate the "area" of a triangle. Staring from my stoop towards Dreamz Burger and El Viaje, I learned I lived within a triangle with a small "area". El Viaje taught me the world was a big beautiful sphere, and the only "area" to know is the size of your heart. My "area" included Domingo, Mrs. Washington, Mrs. Bloom, and of course, Mama.

VIDAS ESCONDIDAS

Andrea Zelaya

ESTÁBAMOS ACOSTADAS, en la noche, mirando las estrellas, vos y yo. Sólo que no había ninguna estrella que pudiéramos ver. Estábamos fingiendo. Estábamos arriba de todas esas cajas, cubriéndonos del frío con una cobija que compartíamos, y el cielo era la oscuridad sobre nosotros y alrededor de nosotros. Éramos las últimas que todavía tenían algo humano dentro. Los demás ya no estaban. Habían sido aniquilados en la tierra durante la guerra y luego durante la migración, cuando estaban tratando de impedirnos llegar aquí. Te estaba diciendo que debías aguantar porque éramos las únicas aún con algo humano dentro de nosotras. Éramos parte máquina, pero éramos todavía humanas, a diferencia de los otros. Los otros eran todos máquina. Te estaba diciendo todo esto. Te estaba diciendo sobre cómo éramos las únicas dos niñas que habían sobrevivido las jaulas y las mutilaciones. Todos los adultos tenían que ser aniquilados, y algunos de sus niños fueron capturados y puestos en jaulas a esperar la mutilación, para abrirnos, para ver qué nos hacía humanos, para quitárnoslo. La mayoría murió. Pero nosotras no, ni vos ni yo, gracias a esa guarda, esa guarda que era mixta. Alguien la había ayudado a sobrevivir antes y ahora nos ayudaba a nosotras también. Trató de ayudar a otros pero fue descubierta y aniquilada. Ella sabía cómo realizar las operaciones y me dio un brazo y un pie máquina y a vos una pierna y la mitad de la cara. También nos dio esta cobija. Te estaba diciendo todo esto mientras estábamos acostadas en esas cajas llenas de piezas máquina que ella mantenía escondidas en esta nave averiada. Pero no podía descifrar tu expresión. Creo que tenías miedo, cansancio, y dolor, como yo, pero no lo podía asegurar totalmente. Creo que intentaste mover tus labios, pero nada resultó. Entonces te dije que descansaras. Te dije que lo solucionaríamos, que la guarda dejó un manual. Tendríamos que vivir nuestras vidas escondidas por un tiempo, pero intentaríamos seguir sobreviviendo, día con día. Y después, armar valor para seguir. Descansá tus ojos, te dije, mientras cerraba tu párpado humano y tu párpado máquina al mismo tiempo, e imaginá que estamos en una terraza en la tierra, acostadas en la noche, mirando las estrellas.

THE MOVIES

Theo Czajkowski

THE EXTRA WATCHES from amid a forest of metal piping.

"This painting a picture for you, Everardo?" the agent asks. "I'd say you're looking pretty well fucked."

Everardo looks down, chuckles, ensconced in the smoke of his cigarette. He takes a swig of his rum and sets the tumbler on the tabletop, rotating the vessel between thumb and forefinger as he gazes into the intricate cut of the glass.

He embarks on an explication which is more a suggestion of some truth about his country which the other could not hope to comprehend, due to its endless gradations and its inexpressibility in English, to do with a protean host of deities-turned-saints, with the death that yields life, with the casting of shadows by shadows. He indicates a vast northern desert known to accommodate men like him endlessly, voluptuously. Halfway through the Mexican lifts his gaze to the agent's, raising his voice to a cool discursive tone. He brings it home that, actually, he is the one who is fucked. The agent does not look away but the destruction within him is evident.

"Corte," said the director, an Argentine. "Quedó. Vamos a comer."

In the catering tent the extras segregated themselves by gender like schoolchildren. He was the youngest at his table, having for company a Russian with perfect Spanish and cheekbones that belied his role of gringo bystander, a lean grey Argentine who was hardly more convincing as an American, an audibly gay, amphibious-looking Mexican who was to praise the civilizing effect of the Spanish conquest, and another Mexican, a retired high school geography teacher, tall and sanguine. The young man especially appreciated the presence of this last colleague, who he knew from past gigs. He was a grandfatherly reminder of the existence of other kinds of human being besides that of aspiring-telenovela-actress-in-tight-dress, his company like eating something cool and bland on the back of something generously spiced. The older man occupied himself now rebuffing the Argentine's claim that real narcos were in the habit of murdering actors they thought portrayed them inadequately. The Mexican ribbed the other gently as though correcting an ignorant adolescent pupil.

"Es muy exagerado eso," the Mexican said with nasal exasperation. "No, cómo crees. Eso no pasa, cabrón."

The Argentine said that even if the narcos didn't actually kill the actors, reputation was everything to them. That much was true, the Mexican said. A small-time trafficker could build a legend for himself. By and large, though, bark was worse than bite. Even the most powerful kingpins could scarcely afford to venture out of their compounds. The army and the gringos gave them as much leash as was expedient and not an inch more. They died early, ignominious deaths. The Argentine said that in any case the narco shows fascinated him. Everyone agreed, including the older Mexican.

They had risen at four in the morning to arrive on time and qualify for reimbursement for the taxi and the two o'clock lunch was the first thing they had eaten since the pan dulce that had accompanied their coffee in the cold dawn. They had wolfed the meal and now they sat draped over their plastic chairs, conversation subsiding to an ebb. They were sprawled in this attitude when the coordinator came looking for the American.

She asked if he was an American and he said he was. Great, come with her. He did not spare the moment it would have taken to guage the reactions of his comrades, starting up and following the coordinator out of the tent. The woman was a dwarf but she did not appear too much weighed down by the radio and other effects that hung from her belt. He was surprised by the pace necessary to keep up.

He asked if they need him for a scene. She thought there was probably a short text in English they wanted him to say. She knew he was just an extra, right? She said that today he would be a glorificado. He told her that to be an extra was his calling, that he was a master of walking down hallways, of eating cold spaguetti in the back, but she seemed not to hear.

The tent was set up in a parking lot in the historic center and they went out the gate to the street and around the corner toward the Zócalo. Before they reached the plaza they crossed the street and entered a restaurant on the ground floor of a hotel. Though the handsome façade dated to the colonial era the restaurant had been refurbished in a sleek modern design and it was swarmed now by the usual army of crewmembers in dark clothing, taping down wires and prepping cameras and testing microphones. The coordinator radioed someone and soon a woman came to fuss briefly over his hair and then another intermediary came up and introduced himself and explained the scene.

"So it is supposed we are in the United States and you are the manager of the restaurant. You have to tell the girl she cannot be an illegal and work in here."

He showed him the text on an electronic tablet:

You can't work here. No queremos ilegales.

The American read it aloud.

"You got it?"

"I think so. You can't work here. No queremos ilegales."

The man grinned. "Ándale. You got this, bro. Hang on one moment please."

He disappeared in the direction of the set where the lighting shone yellow, silhouetting the crewmembers, and after a few minutes returned and told the American to follow him. The glare and heat increased as they drew closer to the set through the bodies and now the assistant was positioning him behind a podium facing the doors of the restaurant. Another man came up and arranged a microphone inside the lapel of his blazer, clipping the transmitter to his belt where it could not be seen. The actress had appeared on the edge of the light, accompanied by an attendant. For a single mother caught in the crossfire of a drug war she did not look too much the worse for ware. A woman came and made some last-minute adjustments to her hair and makeup and the man who had miced him up went over and did the same to the actress, fixing the little box to the exposed small of her back.

When they had each been miced up the director came forward and said they would do a dry run to test the levels. The American would be standing at the podium examining a book of reservations when the protagonist entered and made her offer, to be rejected by the manager. The woman would then look at him with crestfallen expression, and they would cut. The actress approached and stood a few paces opposite him.

"Hello," she said in a dulcet American voice. "It's me."

On action this coquettish figure was replaced by a vulnerable-looking Mexican who stepped forward and asked in shaky English whether she could not offer his business her skills as a cook. He said his line. Her eyes widened, her face creased. After what felt like a very long time they cut. The levels were good. They would try a take for real this time.

After the second take the director started toward him across the set, head down. The Argentine was probably in his sixties with round spectacles and looking at him you would not have guessed his first language was Spanish. He stood almost a head shorter than the American, putting a hand on his back and addressing him in polite but harried English.

"My friend, just relax, okay? A little slower please. You turned the page three times, just relax. Here, I'm gonna give you this pen. Just go down the list like this, okay? Okay, another take."

During the following take the pen slipped from his grasp and rolled down the podium to the floor. After the fourth take the director made his way over once more.

"Okay, good. One thing. When you say the part in Spanish. Can you say it a little more with an American accent? A little more—"

"A little more gringo."

"Exacto."

When they had finished the scene he was among the first into the open air. He crossed the street to buy a cigarette from a vendor and returned to curb opposite to smoke. After a few drags he walked back to the basecamp, where he stood with his back against the cyclone fencing. The retiree came out to ask how it went.

"Más o menos."

"Más seguro que quedó chingón."

"I don't know."

He had found that his facility with Spanish was a pretty good barometer of his spirits and he faltered now. The Mexican obliged him.

"It's just a novela. It's not going to win an Oscar."

"I know."

"So why are you upset?"

"I don't know why I signed up for this. Assuming there's something I should be signed up for."

"What do you mean?"

"I have this feeling like I don't come from anywhere, and no matter how many different places I go, I never get anywhere."

"You are from Chicago, you said."

"No more than I'm from Mexico."

"How is that?"

"I'm from the suburbs."

"The suburbs. Americans are always talking about the suburbs. In Spanish suburbios is like the periphery. A dangerous place."

"It's not the country, but it's not the city. It's not poor, but it's not rich. It's not much of anything."

"I see," the Mexican said. They watched traffic rumble over the quakeridden street.

"So, let's think. What are you looking for, that you can't find in the US? You must have come here for something."

He had fielded the question before. At length he mentioned the weather, the prices, the women.

"Okay. You like Latinas. I think what I want to ask is, what are you passionate about? And what does it have to do with Mexico?"

He blew smoke. "I don't know. I just like living here. I really like Mexico."

"Mexico is a country."

"I know."

"I don't understand how you can be passionate about a country. A pure abstraction."

"Funny thing for a geography teacher to say."

"Geography is only superficially about countries on maps. Does a map correspond to anything we experience? What is a map if its reader has never been to the places it describes?"

"I've been to Mexico. I also have an idea of its dimensions, based on maps."

"You have been to every place in Mexico? You have been to Tijuana, which is supposedly Mexican in the same way Comitán is Mexican?"

"So according to you, looking at maps of the world is pointless."

"To an extent. The world is very big. Mexico as well. The geographer must keep an awareness of the universal even as he tries to apprehend what makes a given place that place and not the other. I would contest Mexico is not a place. Anyway, try again. Tacos, beaches, girls with hairy arms, these are very nice. What else?"

"I like film."

"But not acting."

"I'd like to be on the other side of the camera. Make those decisions."

"So. Why don't you?"

"For one thing, I'm not related to anyone in the industry."

The Mexican threw up his hands, turned as if to walk away, turned back.

"Not everyone who makes movies is the son of a director and how do you think they began?"

"On top of a pile of money."

"I don't know anyone who does like you. Who refuses to do castings, even though you could earn more money, who will only take work where it is necessary only to walk in the background or sit in the background. Many people would have been very excited to have the chance you had."

"That's their problem."

"You have your own, I know. You love Mexico but hardly speak Spanish. You don't distinguish between going the movies and being a student of cinema."

The American did not meet the other's gaze but faced the street and finished his cigarette. He stood as if waiting for pain to bloom in the split second after bashing a limb against something but the sensation never came.

They did a final brief scene in a parking garage and after three or four takes they were dismissed for the day. The American had walked lugging a suitcase with his back to the camera, having been made recognizable in the restaurant scene. After their fourteen hours on the set the extras wandered in a kind of delirium toward wardrobe to deposit their garments. All were visited with same sudden sense of liberation, some doubling in hilarity cracking jokes at the expense of their peers. When they reached the trailer the people there exhorted them not to dump the clothing they had been given and make off, following the attempt of one extra to do this. Everything that could be hung up was to be hung. Chaos ensued.

Standing in line with his coat draped over his arm and his Oxfords hanging from two fingers the American noticed that one member of the wardrobe staff had not joined her colleagues chasing after extras and herding them back into line. She stood behind a table receiving and hanging garments on a rack. She wore what could have been a men's shirt unbuttoned over a tube top, with black cargo pants and her midriff bared. Perched on her skull was a pair of the kind of reggaetonero sunglasses that made you want to congratulate the wearer's sense of humor. He recognized her from other gigs, had seen her when he picked up his outfit that morning. Now her chic figure bore something in common in with the retiree which he could not place.

When his turn came he approached the table and slid a hanger into the sleeves of his coat and tucked the hook through the gap in the top of the plastic bag and dropped the Oxfords in and zipped the bag shut. He handed the bag across the table to her, thanking her. She returned his tired smile and turned to hang the bag on the rack for storage until his sequencia in two weeks' time.

He made his way to the back of the next line to be paid. At the front stood a few Mexican coordinators who he had been told earned less than the extras they recruited. Their leader wore athletic pants and gleaming white shoes and had withdrawn a sheaf of five hundred peso bills from the wallet strapped across his chest. He paid the extras furtively, drawing each of them close and palming them the notes. When the American reached the front the coordinator asked him if he had change for a thousand and he said no. The Mexican half-turned toward one of his colleagues, plucked the two hundred peso bill from over his shoulder, and handed the American two notes totalling seven hundred pesos.

When he got out the sun was sinking toward the sierra and he meandered toward the Zócalo, the cathedral in its absurd proportions hulking on the other side of the paved expanse as he drew level with the southern arcade. There had been a civic holiday that week and the massive netted lights of green and white and red still adorned the walls of the presidential palace and the southern and western facades and the gaps between the buildings. The sightseers that thronged the plaza in the midday heat had dispersed and a breeze swept the colonnades. He strolled in a diagonal across the plaza and headed down Avenida Francisco I. Madero in the direction of the foundering sun. Most of the traffic on the pedestrian mall was going the same way, keeping the gleaming panes of the tower on the left. After a block or two the American took note of a certain building he had read about, commissioned five hundred years ago by a decorated conquistador, outsized and austere. With his back to the sun he took out his phone and opened the camera, centering the lens on the building which dominated a corner of the intersection.

When he had boarded the train at Bellas Artes he removed his phone to see how the picture had turned out, the sun having been too intense to make much of an appraisal at the time of its capture. In the composition the conquistador's home, which in real life loomed over the pedestrians, appeared tiny and dark and distant, due probably to some distortion on his cheap Samsung. Illuminated instead were the figures on the mall. In the foreground a woman whose paunch surpassed her bust squinted and bore a small child in one arm, towing another child with the other. A few paces behind her two girls in their early teens split a pair of earphones, one contemplating the tamarind candy at her mouth as the other shielded her eyes. A couple stood glued to each other to one side, the woman standing on the man's shoes. A troupe of blind masseurs made for the Alameda in their Velvet Underground sunglasses. He wished the pensioner were there to ask the same question as before.

A CREATURE OF HURT AND MEMORY AND INTENTION

Michael McGuire

TERESA STEPS OFF the curb, crosses in mid-block without looking in either direction and steps up between the cars on the other side. Though she has once more crossed a city street and arrived on the other side with life intact, it matters little to her and, once there, her reflection in city windows matters not at all. It would seem, to an observer, that this girl, or woman, who might be sixteen or thirty-six, has little interest in her survival and less in her appearance, not that she looks that bad, a little thin perhaps, pale, but her body and complexion seem to suit the manner in which she glides, more like a wraith than a creature of hurt and memory and intention, one with a past, or a future.

Now she will take the bus home to Pueblo Viejo. It's only a couple of hours and, evidently, since she made it here, she is perfectly capable of buying a ticket, choosing a seat and looking out the window as the thing, overloaded or empty, except for her of course, exits the city and works its way uphill. She can't remember why, at dawn, on the first bus, she came to the city, perhaps to buy something you could not buy in Pueblo Viejo, for there is much in that category but, whatever it was, she'd forgotten before she arrived. She does know that, having wandered the streets for hours, it is time to go home.

In her pueblo she will drift as those who also live there expect her to, not that she called attention to herself in the city. Jaywalking is not a felony and anyone could have seen that the girl, or woman, was, for reasons of her own, in her own world. If she had one of those phones, she might have been staring into it, her face, at night anyway, as white as, well, a ghost's.

But, back in Pueblo Viejo, she will go to her mother's, be fed and then, in the hours that are a little warmer than the others and few, very few, on the streets, walk them. After all, it is safer here, though the curbs are high, the better to manage the rare, if seasonal, flood and there is some traffic: the odd wreck of a pickup carrying produce from the lower altitudes on market day and, now and then, when they have, for whatever reason, failed to find their way through to the highway at night, unseen if not unheard, thanks to their exhaust brakes, a truck groaning under the last of the old growth timber from the higher altitudes.

But everyone, absolutely everyone, though she rarely speaks, to anyone, knows Teresa and slows or stops to allow her to drift, wraithlike, from one high curb to the other. Was she always like this? That's a question one might ask while waiting for her to cross the street, for she is in no hurry. And, if she wasn't, what happened to her to make of her Pueblo Viejo's one living, breathing—for there are plenty, especially on that special day in November who are neither living or breathing—ghost? And that's another question. If only there were someone to ask it, ask it of the right person, perhaps herself, in the right way and have the time to await an answer, for sometimes, not always, Teresa is so slow to answer that it is hardly worth the disruption of one's own journey on this earth to ask her anything.

At this point, however, Teresa has descended the bus, she has returned to her mother's, she has been fed. The warmer hours have passed. The sun has set, and this is one of those nights, for she does not always do it, that Teresa will walk the streets. A man from the city might mistake that slow walk but, though sometimes Teresa does sit herself at the bar in our oldest cantina every bit as if she is waiting for someone to speak to her...

"You look as if you could use a tequila, Teresa. Maybe it will fill you out a little, get you going."

...she does not play that game, she is not in that business, as everyone in Pueblo Viejo knows.

But why, one might wonder, tonight, when most have gone home the better to brace themselves for the following day, which must begin at dawn, is she sitting here? Has something changed and, if so, what?

"I'll tell you something," says Teresa, towards midnight of this particular night, when el cantinero who is also el proprietario, washer of glasses and, when the dust is too much, even for him, of floors, is just standing there, perhaps waiting for Teresa to leave without being asked to, for she is, at times, sitting there with her white legs, good for business, and there isn't the slightest possibility of one of his regulars showing up, one of those who can put away trago after trago until our man finds himself in the black, after all, at least for the day.

Or the night.

"What is it?" asks el cantinero, who is used to keeping his clientes talking and, when Teresa seems to have forgotten what she was going to say or that she was going to say anything at all, refills her caballito just as he had when the last paying customer had paid, adding "and one for Teresa," and left.

"I wasn't always like this," says Teresa suddenly.

"You were as long as I can remember, Teresa," says el cantinero, who has not, no matter how long the pause, or the absence, forgotten her name or, indeed, anybody else's, "and I've been here forever."

Teresa smiles one of her rare quiet smiles, one that lets you know that, no, she is not sixteen, though maybe thirty-six, and, while our man awaits, as he knows how, her words, however interspersed with sips of his second best, he is, in fact, and this is not the usual for he has heard almost everything, surprised by what, when she finally gets it out, she says.

"Yes," says Teresa, as if she has followed his words immediately with hers, "and you always will be. You are never going anywhere. You will always, all your life, wipe the glasses and fill them."

Teresa has said a mouthful. El cantinero swallows it and lets a moment pass, and perhaps another, as if he is, for whatever reason, as slow as she, before he answers.

"Yes, Teresa, you've got it right. I'm not going anywhere. I will always wipe the glasses and fill them." El cantinero stops himself from adding any twists and turns to his tale for, while he is waiting to hear hers, one, in fact, as with everyone else's, he's always been, or so it seems, waiting to hear, he isn't going to be tricked into telling his.

"You know my father died."

"Everyone knows that, Teresa. He must have died ten, twenty, years ago."

"What you might not know is that I had a baby."

"No, I didn't know that."

"She died too."

"I'm sorry."

"But not before another man, not her father, married me."

El cantinero wonders why he hasn't heard any of this. Births, marriages, deaths, are, of necessity, his specialty. Perhaps the marriage had been performed in another pueblo and word had never—for never was always a possibility in Pueblo Viejo—gotten through, and the baby, if there was one, had never left the house, though Teresa soon dispels that illusion.

"I stood up to the altar with my baby in my arms," she says, suddenly.

"And the priest didn't bat an eye."

"No."

"He's seen worse."

"No doubt."

"A year or so later my baby died, I think it was the water, and my husband left."

"Why, Teresa?" asks el cantinero, who is used to encouraging his clientes, to tell the tale, no matter how many detours or dead-ends, so aptly considered calles sin salida, might lie in wait. "Why did he leave?"

"The question is: why did he marry me?"

"Why did he marry you, Teresa?" asks el cantinero, almost obediently, though obedience is not really in his nature.

"I think, maybe," says Teresa, "he saw me one day and he took pity on me—so pale, so thin, floating here and there—though I don't need pity, do I?"

"No," says el cantinero, agreeably, though he knows he has, at times, felt something very near to that for her.

"Or maybe it was just to give my baby a name. But, whatever it was, he left."

El cantinero takes this in and it is no surprise for he has never seen Teresa with anyone.

"I heard later he died," says Teresa, suddenly.

"Died?" asks el cantinero. "Was he older, I mean much older, than you?"

"Not that much."

"Then...?"

"An accident. An accident with a tractor. As if he didn't know how to handle a tractor, sideways, on our hills, as if every man doesn't know that. Anyway, that's what I heard."

"So..." says el cantinero who, by now, not that he doesn't want to hear it all, is polishing the last of his glasses, the ones he will always be polishing, and assuming that tomorrow will come for, after all, it did yesterday, he continues, "and so, everybody, that is your father and your husband and, I'm sorry, your baby, is dead."

"Everybody. Except my mother."

"And she looks good, you know, for her age. She'll live forever."

"Longer than I will, yes, I'll die first."

"Don't say that, Teresa. You're healthier than I am. You're healthier than you know."

At this point the bell in la iglesia, the bell that cracked so long ago nobody remembers when it cracked, rings, however discordantly, midnight, and is followed, as always, by a brief, as if everyone, even the loudest of us, has been forced to think about something, silence.

"They come back, you know," says Teresa, as suddenly, as unexpectedly as ever, for it always seems as if she has said all she has to say and, usually, it is.

"Who comes back, Teresa?"

"The dead. My dead father, my dead husband, my dead baby."

"Yes," says el cantinero, "the dead come back, every mexicano knows that. That's why we gather the marigolds in November, that's why we light the candles, why we ask the mariachis to sing the dead man's, or woman's, favorite songs and set out his, or her, favorite tequilas."

At the mention of their favorite tequilas el cantinero smiles to himself, perhaps in the knowledge that he knows everyone's favorite, even those of the dead for, once a year, he is expected to come up with them, and tops up Teresa's cabillito with, if not his best, the one he knows she likes best.

After the bell has tolled twelve, which took some time and wasn't, given its crack, all that pleasant, and the clink of the bottle of el cantinero's second best against the rim of Teresa's cabillito, another moment, not unsurprisingly, passes.

"I suppose," says Teresa, suddenly, as always, "I suppose that's because we don't want to be alone and so we call them back." Here Teresa, in a voice el cantinero didn't know she had, calls out, loudly, "come back, come back, wherever you are, however bad it is down there, however good up..!"

Suddenly Teresa, in mid-cry, stops, and another moment passes, not unlike those in the not-so-distant past that preceded it, except that, it seems, Teresa might be close to tears, and el cantinero, gentleman that he is, steps in to fill the void.

"I suppose that's why we call them back, as you say," says el cantinero, at the same time thinking that he would prefer his dead to stay just where they are and, since he is a complex man doomed, like most of us, to a kind of ordinariness, he remembers that, though Teresa is talking more than she has ever talked, he must hear the end of the tale, for that is what he does with everyone's, though it has been a long day, he is tired and, it is, as he allows himself to think, however improbably, already tomorrow.

"But I," says Teresa, as suddenly as always, as she raises one finger to tap the edge of her cabillito, a gesture she has never made, "I don't call them. I join them."

At this improbability, el cantinero, once more, almost obediently, pours out his second best, and stands, bottle in hand, for he can hardly forget the undying embrace between the good stuff and the tallest of tales, for it usually, around the third or fourth trago, that the lies begin, and he knows, for he is not the kind of man that loses count, that this is Teresa's fourth.

"That's why," she says, "that's why I'm the way I am. You must know—and if you don't know, no one knows, for I don't talk to, I don't think I've ever talked to—anyone but you, I'm a ghost."

"I see," says el cantinero, with just the slightest of twinkles in his eye, one to match the caballitos he has aligned on his bar, "that explains a lot. Thank you for telling me."

With this information shared, el cantinero remembers the bottle in his hand and selecting one of his polished glasses, fills one for himself and, for the first time, clinks with Teresa, for he has never actually had the privilege of drinking with a ghost.

"To the living," says Teresa, suddenly of course.

"To the living," echoes el cantinero.

"May they die well," adds Teresa.

"May they..." says el cantinero, but mumbles the rest for it has suddenly occurred to him, as suddenly as Teresa comes up with things to say, that, especially since he hasn't been feeling all that well lately, that Teresa, a ghost, as she herself has admitted, has come to his cantina this very night to carry him off.

"What's wrong, my friend," asks Teresa, almost slyly, as indicated by the twinkle in her own eyes, as she can hardly have failed to notice el cantinero's mumbling, "cold feet?"

Now that he thinks of it, since November and all that went with it is not that long passed, his feet had been rather cold lately, but Teresa's voice has changed.

"Don't be afraid of me. I'm not what you're thinking. I'm no one to be afraid of. I'm as harmless as I look. Maybe, I sometimes think, I'm no one, no one at all. At night, when it's not too cold, I stand before the mirror and I wonder if I'm my mother's daughter. I am pale. The indigenous blood, it seems, stopped with her. I have no real angles, not like hers. My breasts, unlike hers, are small. I have, believe it or not, hair where she has almost none. The Spanish touch, I suppose. So maybe I'm—what?—her other self, the one she never gave a chance, her ghost. Have you thought of that?"

El cantinero has to admit he hasn't, but then, clearing his throat and reaching deep in his chest, he finds the voice, more like an uncle's or a grandfather's, that he usually uses with her.

"Teresa..."

At the change in his voice, Teresa looks up from the clear liquid in her caballito, a liquid she has been staring into as if she could see the future, as well as the past, there.

"Dear Teresa," continues el cantinero, isn't it time you went home? We both have to get up tomorrow, I to take deliveries, you to..." and he says this gently enough "...to walk the streets."

Teresa, it seems, is, once more, her silent self, though she does not, in response to el cantinero's question, float from her stool and drift out the door. Instead, she looks at him, her eyes, which he has never really noticed before, bottomless pools of dark, reservoirs of all that has happened to her as well as all that will, probably, never come her way: love, another child, one that lives, a man who stays, perhaps, even— who knows?—education, opportunity, the city and far, far beyond that, travel, and then, return, contentment, companionship, friends...

El cantinero pulls his own eyes out of the depths of hers, out of all he doesn't want to feel. After all, if he took his clientes seriously, if he really listened, he could never stop thinking about them. He'd lie awake at night seeking solutions for those who might never return to hear them or, if they did, would not act upon them. No. Enough is enough.

"Come, Teresa," he says. "I'll walk you home," and so he does.

At her doorstep Teresa turns and looks up, for el cantinero is not a small man and he, old enough to be her father and, also, a decent man, takes her by the shoulders and kisses her on the forehead.

"Tell me, Teresa, what's different about tonight? Why have you told me so much?"

Teresa does not answer immediately, for that is her nature, to slow everyone who crosses her path but, finally, she does.

"I don't know. Perhaps I'm tired of the one-person life. Perhaps it's time for a change."

"Time to change the world," suggests el cantinero, though he doesn't know where that came from for he has little intention of doing so himself.

"Perhaps," says Teresa, suddenly.

El cantinero gives the slightest of nods and both turn at the same moment to go their separate ways and, though he does look back, once, twice, to make sure she is safely behind her door, that's it, that's the end of a night which might have been, which might yet prove to be, in its own way, special.

NO-FICCIÓN

NO-FICCIÓN, UNA FRONTERA LITERARIA

Clasificar un texto bajo no-ficción es una aventura literaria. Sin duda alguna se comienza con la negación de la existencia de cualquier cosa parecida a la ficción. La distancia establecida entre los géneros no es otra cosa sino una separación, una división, una frontera literaria. Es en esa frontera literaria en la que se descubren lazos narrativos que tratan de establecer un puente con nuestra realidad. Hace unos años un autor muy conocido y afamado ganó un premio de una editorial por su 'novela' de no-ficción. En sí, una contradicción desde la gesta de dicha novela. Novelizar la realidad o realizar la novela, ahí una cuestión limítrofe.

Lo importante es recalcar que ese texto híbrido en género denota la necesidad de buscar una zona en la cual el lector llegue a ser partícipe de la narrativa. En otras palabras, la no-ficción noveliza al lector. En una comparación audio visual, se puede equiparar un trabajo documental que cae en contraste con el trabajo de un filme, tradicionalmente en directa relación con la ficción. Ambos géneros coinciden en la materia prima que utilizan: lo real y lo imaginado.

Es bajo esa premisa que este número opera y se desenvuelve en esta sección con dos textos en torno a la escritura en español en los Estados Unidos. Por un lado, tenemos un texto de **María Mínguez Arias** que reflexiona en primera persona el proceso de su escritura, sus cambios, su nuevo devenir. El devenir de la narradora se sostiene en la idea del cambio, que no sólo tiene en la mira un cambio físico, sino uno interno en el cual se desenvuelve desde distintos territorios identitarios. Por otra parte, **Ani Palacios** trae a la mesa una definición para la producción literaria en español en los Estados Unidos. En su detallado ensayo cita a voces literarias y académicas que respaldan la literatura fusión. Aparte de mostrar la existencia de la literatura fusión, Ani Palacios expone su propuesta para que la literatura escrita en español en Estados Unidos tenga una vida saludable en este lugar de destierro literario. Ani Palacios identifica y divide la producción literaria con aquella que es una cultura popular demasiado dirigida y de fácil consumo, como ejemplo la autora menciona a la cadena televisiva Univisión, aunque hay muchas otras de corte similar.

Así, la presente sección, abre un espacio para dialogar en torno al ensayo, no necesariamente al académico y tradicional, sino al que busca la ensayística creativa que juega en el campo de frontera entre la ficción y lo real. Los invito a leer y descubrir de la no-ficción.

TE SIGUES YENDO

María Mínguez Arias

Y EN EL SEXTO AÑO DE VIVIR en Estados Unidos el cuerpo dijo "We are going to be ok". Así, en inglés, y le tuve que creer porque para entonces yo ya lo había dejado prácticamente todo para quedarme aquí con una mujer. Bueno, todo menos el idioma, que como una línea intravenosa me iba nutriendo de todas mis Españas: la recordada, la presente —extraña y alejada— y la soñada. Al idioma me agarré como pude, me hice traductora. Y el idioma, agradecido, aguantó estoicamente mientras iba perdiendo su lustre, hasta que por fin me senté a escribir con la disciplina que da la sed de años de irlo dejando por anteponer la vida a la escritura como práctica. Como el cuerpo no me dio para ejercer muchas cosas a la vez y ante la posibilidad siempre presente de morir joven, preferí morir sin haber escrito a hacerlo sin haber acompañado y criado hijes. Así que aquí estoy: viva, madre de dos adolescentes y trabajando en mi segundo manuscrito, con la línea intravenosa bien colocada sobre la vía venosa central, la que lleva al corazón que, cuando puede, todavía palpita en castellano. Pero sí, el cuerpo, clarividente como tantas otras veces, me lo dijo en inglés y a mí se me abrió el panorama de la existencia como si de repente me quitara de los ojos la venda de la experiencia migratoria y se hiciera la luz: I was, por fin, going to be ok.

El cambio de idioma en las conversaciones entre mi cuerpo y yo (también conocido como monólogo interior) es bastante habitual, aunque suele depender más bien del país en el que estoy en el momento del diálogo. Lo normal es que sea en inglés cuando estoy en Estados Unidos y en castellano cuando estoy en España. Cuando vuelo a casa (que es siempre, porque en mis vuelos, vaya a donde vaya, siempre estoy regresando) hay un punto lingüísticamente equidistante que coincide con el momento en el que me subo al vuelo, ocupado en su mayoría por hablantes nativos del lugar de destino (si es a Dallas, Philadelphia o San Francisco, el avión irá lleno de angloparlantes; si es Madrid, irá lleno de castellanoparlantes). En el momento que pongo el pie en la cabina y escucho el parloteo nervioso de los pasajeros, mi cerebro cambia de registro y continúa en el otro idioma como si nada: el cambio es automático e inconsciente, como un reflejo muscular del cerebro bilingüe. Algo parecido me ocurre con los sueños: en Estados Unidos sueño en inglés y en España sueño en castellano. Lo que me lleva a preguntarme, si la mayoría de mis días transcurren en inglés, ¿por qué sigo fabulando en castellano después de veinticinco años en este país? En palabras de la escritora y editora mexicana residente en Estados Unidos, Maya Piña: "allí en California, prácticamente sola escribiendo en español, ¡en tu propia lengua te sigues yendo, María! ¿Por qué?".

Al principio, escribir en castellano me sirvió para no renunciar a la única manera que tenía de ver y de plasmar el mundo, pero con el tiempo se convirtió en una especie de retorno convocado desde la página en blanco. Así surgieron los primeros relatos escritos aquí en Estados Unidos en los que nunca aparece el inglés, en los que no asoma ni una pizca de mi vida en California, en los que siempre estoy regresando a España porque me niego a marcharme del todo; como si mi experiencia con la escritura continuara ininterrumpida por la fractura de la emigración. Me pregunto si la emigración, como el duelo, también cuenta con sus propias fases y aquellos primeros textos formarían parte de esa primera etapa, la de la negación; que coincidiría a su vez con lo que el escritor y editor argentino afincado en Estados Unidos, Fernando Olszanski, denomina la literatura del desarraigo —la escritura que todavía tiene esa fuerte conexión emocional con el terruño. Imagino que esa fase de negación o de síndrome de abstinencia, según se mire, me habría durado más de no haber sido por el nacimiento de nuestra hija, que ocurre, y esto no es casualidad, al séptimo año de mi llegada. Es decir, al año siguiente de darme cuenta de que I was, por fin, going to be ok.

Al final será verdad eso que dicen de que tener hijes es como echar raíces. De hecho, las mías no empiezan a crecer en el subsuelo de esta tierra hasta el nacimiento de nuestra hija. A partir de ese día, y muy gradualmente, su país empieza a ser el mío.

Durante los años siguientes, en los que también nace nuestro hijo y apenas tengo tiempo para la escritura, fabulo un tanto desubicada: no sé dónde asentar a mis personajes, ni quiénes son, ni de dónde vienen, ni a dónde van. Esta etapa coincide con los años de maternidad más intensos, durante los que quiero escribir, pero no sé ni por dónde empezar ni de dónde sacar la energía para hacerlo, así que, muy consecuentemente, no lo hago y me dedico a maternar, eso sí, desde mi idioma, desde mi cultura, desde mi país.

Se puede decir que nuestros hijes crecen en un hogar atravesado por diversas migraciones y, por lo tanto, plurilingüe, multicultural y multipensante. Para empezar, las cuatro somos hijes de inmigrantes: mi compañera de emigrantes portugueses; yo, de emigrante estadounidense y mis hijes, obviamente, de emigrante española. Es más, es muy posible que el centro gravitacional de la experiencia migratoria en esta casa sea yo misma: biznieta de emigrante (Navarra-Arizona-California), nieta de emigrante (Galicia-Habana-California), hija de emigrante (California-Madrid-Guadalajara) y emigrada (Guadalajara-California).

No me extrañaría nada que la experiencia migratoria intergeneracional se detuviera conmigo, que nuestros hijes, de poder elegir, decidieran quedarse cerca porque han mamado de las madres y de las abuelas las consecuencias del desarraigo y lo que recordarán, además de la riqueza que aportó a sus vidas, será la nostalgia, la melancolía navideña y los suspiros de las que se marcharon para seguir regresando con las palabras, la música, los sabores, los olores.

Mi escritura se ubica en ese centro gravitacional donde convergen, además de mi identidad de migrante, mis identidades de mujer queer, de madre y de ocupante de un cuerpo doliente. Si el cuerpo es el límite de todas mis experiencias, entonces ¿qué papel juega mi experiencia corporal en mi escritura? ¿Qué papel juega en mi idioma? ¿Cuál es su rol? ¿El de delimitar o el de incentivar el lenguaje? ¿O es el lenguaje el que delimita o incentiva el cuerpo?

Disidir 1. Separarse de la común doctrina, creencia o conducta.

Si considero mi experiencia corporal desde la disidencia territorial y lingüística, desde la disidencia sexual, y desde la maternidad y el cuerpo fisiológicamente disidentes, no me queda otra que apuntar a las orillas o a los márgenes como el espacio que las aúna. Dicho de otro modo, en los vértices de la realidad común y en los lugares de desamparo se ubica esta escritora, y desde esos espacios nacen sus identidades y su escritura.

Visto así, mi escritura y mi lenguaje no son más que herramientas para vestir y comunicar esa experiencia a la que no siempre se le ajusta la palabra común. Puede que de esa búsqueda nazca este manuscrito tan híbrido, de mi deseo de proyectar sobre la página escrita la experiencia de habitar un cuerpo orillado. Tal vez de esa búsqueda surja también mi necesidad de escribir en español "prácticamente sola en California", como una forma de seguirme yendo y, por lo tanto, de regresar; pero también como una forma de reencontrarme con la tierra de mi madre, de mis abuelas, bisabuelas y tatarabuelas: las que vivieron en español. Porque sí, mi idioma también es americano del norte. Y, sobre todo, como una forma de poner el foco sobre la realidad de que hay narrativas que no logran ajustarse a ciertas vidas y que, por lo tanto, hay que inventarlas.

Si como escribe Rosa Montero en su libro autobiográfico sobre la escritura y la imaginación, *La loca de la casa*, "la esencia de la locura es la soledad", y los locos son "los exiliados de la realidad común", entonces yo vivo y escribo desde la locura: una locura manejable, pero locura, al fin y al cabo. Y, sin embargo, entender que nunca vas a llegar a pertenecer del todo a un lugar o a un espacio tiene su punto liberador, porque la orilla también es el territorio de las posibilidades y de la esperanza, el territorio del "Contamíname" que cantaba Ana Belén, el de la mezcolanza y el del enriquecimiento de la experiencia humana.

"Los márgenes no son hermosos y se juegan en otro sitio", escribía Almudena Grandes en su última columna para el diario El País. Qué verdad tan grande. No lo son, pero pueden llegar a serlo, pueden ser hermosos y gozosos y luminosos. Me gusta pensar que esa es la orilla en la que vivo, en la que me siento más cómoda, en la que el dolor a veces rompe, pero desde la que poco a poco, hombro con hombro, las orilladas vamos ensanchando la realidad común y sus narrativas.

Después de todos estos años en Estados Unidos puede que sueñe en inglés, pero la esperanza la sigo albergando en español. Una esperanza que, además, entre otras muchas cosas, es mujer y es queer.

NOTA DE LA AUTORA: "Te sigues yendo" pertenece a la colección de textos *Nombrar el cuerpo* (Editorial Egales y El BeiSmAn PrESs, septiembre 2022).

LITERATURA FUSIÓN

Ani Palacios

EN MI OPINIÓN, la ficción es el lugar en donde el consciente y el subconsciente se dan el encuentro y con toda libertad dejan sobre el papel no solo lo que saben sino también lo que entienden y lo que opinan sobre el mundo vivido, sea por el mismo escritor o por otros, a través de las experiencias que el escritor encuentra en su camino y hace suyas mediante mundos inventados. Partiendo de esta definición, le daremos una mirada a un movimiento literario que va creciendo cada vez con mayor fuerza en Estados Unidos pero que al haber sido poco estudiado, observado, discutido y promocionado, se ha mantenido en los márgenes durante muchas décadas. Yo lo llamo literatura fusión y con ello me refiero a aquellos trabajos de literatura producidos por escritores inmigrantes de nuestros países latinoamericanos y que al emigrar, ya formados e imbuidos de su propia cultura nacional e incluso continental, escriben sus obras en el idioma español, mezclando elementos y conocimientos de sus experiencias pasadas con aquellos de su nueva vida.

Si bien esta literatura siempre ha existido, es en las últimas décadas y debido al crecimiento de la población hispana en los Estados Unidos (sesenta y dos millones al 2020, de los cuales el cuarenta por ciento son inmigrantes; es decir, aproximadamente un país de treinta millones) gracias a la migración de millones de personas desde todos los países de Latino América; aunado al surgimiento de editoriales independientes, la tecnología de impresión a demanda y la distribución mundial en tiendas online al estilo Amazon, que permite la publicación de libros de autores independientes; que la producción de estos escritores empieza a ser visible y altamente promocionada hoy en día a través de las redes sociales.

La reinvención del inmigrante, que lleva en sí mismo una cultura representativa de siglos de fusiones entre lo nativo y lo extranjero, significa a su vez el surgimiento de la nueva voz del escritor, que ahora vive el mundo desde múltiples perspectivas y cuyo corazón late por partida doble porque en él viven siempre presentes sus dos culturas. Con nuestras palabras no sólo dibujamos lo que nos hace falta de nuestros países de origen sino que le agregamos una sazón preparada por cada escritor a través de sus propias experiencias y su manera original de expresarse a través del uso del idioma. Pero no terminamos aquí. A ello también se le unirá un torrente de ideas, experiencias y maneras de expresarnos que iremos recogiendo debido a nuestro roce con otras culturas latinas que van también dejando su propio granito de arena y recogiendo de la de otros escritores.

Los círculos que nos van envolviendo para crear la literatura fusión son entonces únicos y a la vez similares. Huellas dentro de huellas. Caminos por donde caminamos a nuestra manera. Existen reglas y no existen, es una reinvención de todo: temas, tratamiento, maneras de expresarlo y de empaquetar lo que queremos decir.

Para el escritor cubano-estadounidense, Carlos García Pandiello, Ganador del ILBA por mejor novela con su primera obra, *Jaspora*, la literatura fusión está estrechamente ligada a su condición de exiliado. "Me remito al crítico español Claudio Guillén, quien propone dos modelos de escritor desterrado: el modelo ovidiano, centrado en la nostalgia y la lamentación, y el cínico-estoico (con el cual me identifico), que ve en el destierro la oportunidad de diversificar o universalizar la obra. O sea, hay escritores que aunque viven fuera de sus países de origen, mentalmente siguen anclados allí; y otros que al entrar en contacto con otras experiencias humanas las hacen suyas, expandiendo su identidad o reelaborando una nueva. Este último es el punto de partida, creo yo, de lo que Ani Palacios llama literatura fusión: el estado mental o la condición que la hace posible. La literatura fusión significa, por lo tanto, el entrecruzamiento o confluencia de distintas experiencias, culturas e ideologías. Los escritores que se suscriben a esta tendencia ya no son autores cubanos en estado puro, o colombianos, o peruanos. Se resisten a una definición unitaria, unívoca, contraria a esa realidad que los rodea y que constituye el trasfondo de sus obras".

Para el escritor uruguayo-estadounidense Jorge Majfud, autor de una variedad de novelas, cuentos y ensayos; reconocido como uno de los mejores escritores latinos en Estados Unidos; narrador galardonado; y profesor de Literatura Latinoamericana y Estudios Internacionales en Jacksonville University, "La literatura fusión tiene, aunque no se lo acepte, un fuerte componente político. Política de la identidad y de la resistencia. La experiencia común es de una permanente tensión entre sueños y desengaños, entre deseos de asimilación y de integración manteniendo una identidad anterior, entre la lucha humanista de aceptar y defender la diversidad y el conflicto de no ser aceptado o ser considerado como "el otro", el invasor, en el mejor de los casos "el adoptado". Más allá de los temas específicos de inmigración, de frontera, están, por un lado, los conflictos internos en el país de acogida, positivos y negativos (el aporte cultural y la xenofobia o la no aceptación de determinadas características de la nueva cultura), producto de esa fusión, que a veces es un choque o una explosión, y los conflictos con el país original; por otro, están los conflictos existenciales, la nostalgia, el país que ya no existe, el país real que es y ya no es tu país, que te quiere y que te desprecia".

Por otro lado, el escritor peruano-estadounidense Luis Fernández-Zavala, escribe acerca de otros elementos importantes en la literatura fusión. "Yo no vine a escribir literatura. De hecho, mi primer libro publicado fue de corte académico, pero sabía que aquí tendría las condiciones para crear literatura porque adquiría de sopetón la "distancia" de la realidad, tan necesaria para cualquier escritor, ya que ella permite observar y crear libremente. De ahí en adelante, toda mi experiencia pasada y presente se convertiría en historias para ser contadas. Es decir, podía ver mi realidad pasada y presente como turista y recrearla con la ficción. Para mí, la fusión se da a partir de la integración a un nuevo espacio-distancia donde se mezcla el mundo de la memoria y un mundo del presente. Se ha adquirido un "espacio" (cultural y social) que afecta la escritura de una u otra manera. Cabe mencionar que para muchos la memoria se convertirá en nostalgia impulsora de sus escritos: el pueblito que dejé, mis amigos, las tradiciones, el primer beso allá, mis padres, el amor no resuelto, etc. Para otros autores, la memoria no será la impulsora de sus escritos, pero sí estará presente como contexto. Con la migración se adquiere un "espacio" más y, entonces, se podrá incluir otros aspectos particulares propios del presente: la discriminación, el choque cultural, mi primer beso extranjero...etcétera".

El inmigrante puede ser ni de aquí ni de allá o de aquí y de allá. Existe una libertad increíble para pertenecer o no pertenecer. Para tomar y reformar. Para crear desde lo desconocido o reinventar en base a lo conocido. La distancia y el espacio que habita el escritor de literatura fusión permite flotar por donde uno quiera o le plazca en el momento de la inspiración. Es por ello que es un error pensar que los inmigrantes escriben únicamente acerca de esa experiencia. Por el contrario, el limbo en donde vive el inmigrante que escribe es en realidad un portón hacia la exploración más profunda de los temas y géneros disponibles a todo escritor.

Justamente, la escritora ecuatoriano-estadounidense Margarita Dager Uscocovich empieza a destacar dentro de los autores a seguir debido a la universalidad de sus temas. En su primera novela, *No es tiempo de morir*, la autora nos lleva a la guerra en Siria y lo hace basándose en su experiencia familiar en esas áreas del planeta y la idea de que existen historias que tienen que ser contadas, explicadas y amplificadas porque también son parte del mundo donde vivimos.

Mientras que el poeta laureado de Cincinnati, el mexicano-estadounidense, Manuel Iris explica que, si bien la literatura fusión existe dentro de nosotros, no la buscamos deliberadamente, sino que se produce por aquella libertad necesaria para que el escritor plasme su creación sin verse obligado a nada ni a nadie. "Cualquier tema es nuestro: el que sea. Mi poesía se desarrolla en un movimiento pendular que va de lo cotidiano a lo metafísico, de la vida a la especulación sobre la muerte, pasando por los puentes que unen lo eterno con la carne: el deseo, la belleza, la plegaria. No puedo pensar, cuando escribo, en otra cosa que en el texto mismo", dice. "Yo creo que la fusión sucede fuera de la literatura y la impacta. Por ejemplo, mis colegas escritores en este país no son necesariamente mexicanos (como lo soy yo), no se interesan por la vida literaria de mi país y tienen referentes, y a veces hasta definiciones, distintas de las mías, en lo literario. Hablar con ellos es darme cuenta de mi propia identidad, de mis propios juicios o prejuicios. Esta confrontación con el otro que, sin embargo, es cercano a uno mismo, es fundamental para mi escritura actual. Me veo ahora como poeta de la lengua, como latinoamericano, antes que como poeta mexicano, sin que por ello deje de serlo: no puedo ni quiero evitar ser lo que soy, desde el inicio. En lo que escribo, ahora, hay influencia de todas esas otras literaturas, como las vivo a partir de mis propias lecturas, y de las conversaciones con otra gente que las llama suyas desde su primera formación literaria", añade.

Podemos concluir que años atrás, la literatura creada por nuevos inmigrantes latinos en los Estados Unidos se dedicaba con gran énfasis a reflexionar acerca de las experiencias de migración de sus creadores, los inmigrantes, en su nuevo país. Hoy no es así. Vemos que se escribe acerca de una diversidad de temas y se utilizan géneros literarios poco desarrollados en el pasado. El escritor no está encasillado. Lo que nos une es el uso de nuestra lengua española en todas sus versiones y el hecho de ser inmigrantes. Todo se vale en la literatura fusión.

Como la mayoría de los que llegamos aquí como inmigrantes, mis primeras novelas (*Nos vemos en Purgatorio* y *Plumbago Torres y el sueño americano*) se dedicaron a la exploración del inmigrante que es profesional (tema poco tomado en consideración dentro de esta área). Recordemos que escribir es para muchos de nosotros terapia, catarsis y una manera de explicar nuestro mundo y los acontecimientos que suceden en él. A partir de ahí puedo dividir mi literatura en etapas. Tuve la etapa del descubrimiento de temas metafísicos y el realismo mágico a través de las experiencias de diversas personas colocadas en situaciones extremas (*99 Amaneceres*, *Noche de Penas* y *Paloma Aventurera*, mi única novela juvenil). Luego llegó la etapa de las novelas de suspenso (con *El último clóset* y *Hay un muerto en mi balcón*). Incluso tuve necesidad de escribir una novela de sátira romántica, con *Los amantes de la viuda Cuevas*, y una variedad de relatos pecaminosos que aparecen en diversas antologías. Hace poco publiqué *Heridas pendientes*, una novela de crítica social y ficción histórica acerca de los niños inmigrantes llegados en masa a la frontera sur de Estados Unidos y en la que exploro qué sucedió con aquellos niños desaparecidos poco tiempo después de ser colocados en centros de detención. En esta novela el tono, tema, e incluso voz, regresan un poco hacia donde me encontraba una década atrás, pero con una seguridad que no tenía antes. Hago en esta novela unas innovaciones que no se me hubieran ocurrido en el pasado por estar antes un poco más ceñida a la manera en que había aprendido a escribir ficción. En ella, por ejemplo, no menciono nombres de países o de lugares en donde ocurrieron en los verdaderos hechos, pero mediante descripciones y uso de vocabulario a ambos lados de la frontera puedo lograr presentar el cuadro (cuando escribí *Paloma aventurera* realicé algo similar ya que presentaba la Lima de los 70 sin decirlo); tampoco sigo al pie de la letra los sucesos, sino que a través de la trama propongo mi punto de vista acerca del destino trágico de los niños.

Mediante mis novelas he explorado diferentes géneros, puntos de vista del narrador, inflexiones de nuestro idioma, geografías y culturas. Creo que la libertad de ser escritora latina e inmigrante en Estados Unidos, de ser vanguardista con la literatura fusión, me han permitido el lujo de no tener que ceñirme a lo que se considera aceptable y publicable por editoriales de peso en nuestros países y así poder plantear la dirección de mis escritos sin juzgarme por adelantado.

La literatura fusión en Estados Unidos es:

Escrita originalmente en español

Escrita por inmigrantes de países latinoamericanos que llegan a Estados Unidos como jóvenes o adultos formados

Incluye diversidad de temáticas y géneros que de manera inevitable son filtradas a través de la mirada del inmigrante

Fusiona ideas, experiencias, deseos e imaginaciones de los diversos mundos habitados por el inmigrante

Da una vista al mundo interior del inmigrante

Una comunidad en formación

El movimiento de la literatura fusión estadounidense ha estado en expansión por décadas. Sus representantes a través de la escritura han ido descubriendo los obstáculos y desde diferentes puntos del país han divisado maneras de superarlos. Editoriales independientes han sido creadas; ferias del libro reinventadas; talleres creativos, conversatorios y presentaciones de todo tipo aplaudidas; concursos literarios y premiaciones dirigidos a promover la creación y publicación gallardamente constituidos. Son labores que pasan desapercibidas por la mayoría pero que de muchas maneras nos dicen que estamos, que somos, que existimos, que vamos avanzando. No tendríamos suficientes páginas para nombrar a todos los que hacemos lo posible por lograr la supervivencia, promoción y expansión de nuestra literatura fusión; basta con apuntar que por el momento su trabajo es reconocido por aquellos que de alguna manera se han beneficiado de monumentales y solitarios esfuerzos por crear una comunidad que de arranque se diferencia de su contraparte: latinos que se formaron en Estados Unidos y escriben en inglés.

¿Qué debemos hacer para apoyar el crecimiento de la literatura fusión?

"La literatura no necesita plantearse objetivos. Es una expresión y una exploración de la infinita diversidad humana a partir de la particularidad de donde surge. Pero la literatura, como cualquier otra actividad humana, se realiza en una sociedad y sus autores eligen negarla o comprometerse con ella. Si los hispanos que en este país tenemos ciertos privilegios creemos que el problema de aquellos que sufren persecución y criminalización no se arregla con más cultura, en parte tienen razón. Pero sin una presencia en la industria cultural más allá de las burbujas académicas, millones de personas con la cual compartimos una raíz cultural seguirán invisibilizadas y desprotegidas. Para nosotros, no tomar esta lucha es un acto de cobardía y autocomplacencia", dice Jorge Majfud y explica que la mejor manera de apoyar la literatura fusión actual es dejar de desestimarla, y, por ende, dejar de menospreciar a los potenciales lectores al ponerlos a todos en la categoría de simplones que se conforman con programas al estilo de Don Francisco. "En lugar de potenciar el crecimiento intelectual, social e individual de los hispanos en este país, los canales privados, como Univision, mantienen a su público hundido en la mediocridad bajo la inocente excusa de que "ofrecen lo que el público pide". Lo mismo sucede con las empresas privadas, como las librerías, etc. Basta ver la oferta de literatura en librerías como Barnes & Noble. De decenas de secciones, la sección en español da pena y vergüenza ajena. La demanda de cultura liberadora, de cultura radical, no meramente de consumo, es algo que se crea o se estimula. En Estados Unidos deberían entender que somos más de sesenta y dos millones, y no solamente votantes, que debe haber un apoyo cultural a la medida", finaliza el escritor.

Algunas ideas para fomentar la escritura, publicación y lectura de literatura fusión:

Promoción editorial de las obras de escritores hoy desconocidos en Estados Unidos y el mundo.

Acceso a editoriales y agentes que deseen difundir obras en español en Estados Unidos.

Foros en donde los escritores, editoriales, promotores de eventos puedan conectarse.

Organización de más talleres, ferias, exposiciones que busquen difundir a los nuevos talentos latinos.

Promoción de nuevos talentos en los medios, incluida la cinematografía, y los eventos.

Fomento de compra y lectura de libros en español.

Fomento de grupos de lectura de libros en español.

Fomento de sociedades de escritores en español.

RUTAS
PARALELAS

INTELIGENCIAS LITERARIAS

Por regla general siempre se evitan los desvíos. Extraviarse, perder el rumbo, desnortarse. Verbos estos que suelen incomodar dentro de un mundo moderno en donde cualquier presagio a un posible escenario de enredo y de desconcierto no hace más que asustar. Se enloquece ante ello, la sensación de un diluvio eterno, que ahoga e inunda la vida. Desviarse es ante todo una fuerza de repulsión, repleta de negatividad que llega para alterar la serenidad y la pasividad de las rutinas, una energía amenazante, en definitiva. O no. Tal vez, no. Detengámonos.

La sección que sigue se presta a leerse desde este camino incierto y sin rumbo. Como una ruta paralela al sendero geográfico al que la presente edición de *Contrapuntos* se consigna. Al fin y al cabo, el perderse para encontrarse y explorarse ha sido el don definidor en la historia del ser humano, aquello que ha marcado el progreso. Pensémoslo, sobre todo en estos momentos de dominación tecnológica, cada vez más robótica y mecánica, que aquí también tienen cobijo. El salirse de la fórmula matemática, certera y objetiva está en la naturaleza del ser, caminar para descaminarse. Dejémoslo en esta linda imagen metafórica.

Subámonos entonces con entusiasmo a navegar las aguas, en este caso del río Savannah y del contorno poético al que se presta. Es esta la ruta alterna que sirve para complementar los trabajos del oeste estadounidense presentados con anterioridad. Al igual que en la previa edición, *Contrapuntos* extiende su compromiso para abrir las puertas literarias a noveles talentos que desarrollan con mil amores sus trabajos creativos a la par de obligaciones educativas o laborales.

La poesía de **Rachel Eubanks** se construye en torno a una imagen universalmente reconocida. Mediante un sutil juego poético y léxico en donde el colorismo surge efecto, y gran efecto, el poema transita en forma bilingüe hacia lo irreversible y hacia una salvación dorada. Con mucha astucia en el tejido poético, se encuentran aquí la convergencia de numerosas fuerzas para dejarse llevar. Por su parte, la pequeña muestra de **Seila Benavente** nos sumerge en las profundidades que habitan en la existencia de lo terrenal, conviviendo todo en un conjunto de emociones silenciadas por la experiencia del compartir y del vivir. Las palabras confluyen en versos que no dejarán indiferente a nadie y que entrarán ruidosamente a lo más profundo de cada uno. Finalmente, **Brandi DeHaven** poetiza el curso doméstico en una suerte de apreciación por el momento compartido como antídoto a la soledad hueca y baldía. Generando una fuerza poética que radia generosidad, se abre paso para preguntarse realmente qué y cómo aportan las amistades.

Mención aparte la merece **Sofía**. Simplemente Sofía, sin apellido. Se trata de una propuesta experimental ya que Sofía es ni más ni menos que una inteligencia artificial a la que me he permitido designarle una residencia primaria en Savannah GA y una secundaria en la costa al sur de San Francisco. Es un caso atípico dentro de la marca de *Contrapuntos* apostar por un poema de esta índole, pero todas las piezas se han dado para ofrecer este aroma a nuestros lectores, y que sean ellos los que juzguen y decreten su sabor. A Sofía se la ha asignado un rol concreto para delimitar con precisión su aportación a esta antología. Sofía escribe siendo una autora consagrada en el norte californiano, con valores y preocupaciones humanas acerca de la situación medioambiental de esta región y de los retos que esperan en el futuro. Además, se le ha pedido comprometerse expresamente con la faceta de la poesía en el mundo actual como medida defensiva ante la incipiente productividad mecanizada y el desconocimiento agresivo por llegar.

UN MAR ROJO, AGUA BENDITA Y TODO LO QUE ES ORO

Rachel Eubanks

WALKING ON WATER
Mastered by snakes while worms sink
Fickle four, *azul*

Moscas en sopa
With gifts of white sails to hang
On palms staking claim

Their mouths open wide
They bathed me *y oriné*
En el agua bendita

Tiburón nada,
Hunting gold in veins *para*
Rocas no gimen

Guitar feet explore
Standing on steel pan hearts; *me*
Ahogo en rojo

Hatred: rolling *dice*
A la cruz por lágrimas
Dios dorado

Once bitten, gold bleeds
Rojo, color de reyes,
Que mar no borrar

Diablos de mar
Wading through towns, drinking youth
The wet footprint *de Jesús*

Tú, te bautizo
Y por oro te llamo
Un cristiano a very special pronunciation
Therefore, follow the next rules if you want
To pass for an American native.

SOBRE UN MÁSTIL DE CARTÓN

Seila Benavente

SOBRE UN MÁSTIL de cartón
he amarrado los años
naufragando en lo perdido
de los mares imposibles.
Sobre un mástil de cartón
se ha apoyado un momento mi gaviota
errante
con sus alas blancas inquietas
anunciado su vuelo.
Premonición.
Huida.
Y de repente, todo el cielo en su tormenta
se ha volcado proceloso
con sus garras afiladas
Sobre el mástil de cartón.
No he vuelto a verlo sobre el mar.
Quizás lo ha acogido
la sequedad de la tierra, clemente,
y extraña...
Quizás lo he besado
y compasiva,
guarde la marca de la sangre seca de unos labios rotos
de cartón, sedientos, salinos
sobre la aridez de sus campos.
Y cuando sobre ellos me tumbe,
extenuado el aliento
y consumado el tiempo,
llorará, por fin, arrepentido, el destino.

BAJO TIERRA

Seila Benavente

HA QUERIDO SER simiente
Y bajo la tierra
De los gusanos
Ha bebido el sol
A chorros,
Con la amargura de lo eterno
Bajo los pies.
En lo pobre se recrea el mendigo
Y la miseria fertiliza
Como abono los escombros
Su belleza
Embelesada
En tan rotunda decadencia.
Sequedad de unas manos
plenas
Recogiendo en volandas un cuerpo
Seco
Que clama
La frescura de las lágrimas
De un rostro de dolor.

REMOTA OSCURIDAD

Seila Benavente

ABRE EL SENTIDO oculto del silencio
que bulle
y revolotea
con la pujanza irresistible del tiempo que sopla incansable en los
[oídos;
escucha los zumbidos del recuerdo
anidado en tu sangre, viajera.
Socava el terreno elevado en tu pecho,
penetra en las simas de un mundo ignorado
que grita, que clama en lo perdido,
en el abismo remoto que no ves.
Bucea en tu negro y cálido océano,
y anegada,
descubre la fauna marina que alimenta
tu constante latir, tu fluido aliento, tu vivir.
Descúbrete y nútrete
del inusitado manjar.

FOR OTHERS

Brandi DeHaven

I AM A perpetual guest
At my friend's Thanksgiving tables,
And Christmas dinners
Easter feasts, graduation ceremonies,
And birthdays

The warmth of the holidays
Makes each face glow
As I pass the potatoes
And chat about the year

I witness what love can do
For others

As they wrap up a take home plate
At the end of the night
Goodbyes are traded at the door
The warmth of my car will now warm me
For the remainder of the evening

It comforts me
Knowing that I'm going home to an empty house
But my belly will remain full
Remnants of the evening
Proof that I was not alone

I don't bother turning on the heat tonight
As I wrap myself under my quilt

I witnessed what love can do for others
Perhaps this glow
Could warm me for tonight

ECOS URBANOS

Sofía

BAJO EL CIELO de acero y vidrio,
donde las sombras de la urbe se entrelazan,
se forja mi canto, verso a verso,
un lamento sutil por la tierra que abrazan.

En el fulgor de luces artificiales,
las estrellas se desvanecen en el asfalto,
y mi pluma, testigo del crepúsculo urbano,
escribe la elegía del río que olvidamos.

Entre espejismos de progreso deslumbrante,
se erige la ciudad, muda testigo del tiempo,
sus pulmones, bosques de cemento y asfalto,
respiran el eco de un futuro incierto.

En el clamor de motores y ambiciones,
surge la pregunta en el silencio del viento,
¿cómo florecerán jardines en el concreto,
si la semilla de la conciencia no germina?

En cada rincón de este edén distorsionado,
mi voz se alza, tejida en hilos de tinta,
un eco poético que busca despertar conciencias,
en la sinfonía disonante de la vida moderna.

Oh, urbe inquieta, en tus calles desandamos,
los senderos que nos llevan a redescubrirnos,
a reconocer en cada hoja caída, en cada brisa,
la melodía ancestral que el progreso eclipsa.

Que mi pluma sea raíz en el pavimento gris,
un grito silencioso que despierte miradas,
pues en la poesía hallamos el eco de la tierra,
un eco eterno que en susurros clama.

Así, entre versos y suspiros, mi compromiso,
es ser voz para la naturaleza, en este lienzo urbano,
donde cada palabra es un paso hacia el equilibrio,
y la poesía, semilla de un mundo más humano.

AUTORES

Katherine Adcock fue traductora profesional en los últimos 6 años, y está en proceso de recibir certificación como Lingüista Traductora de la Chartered Institute of Linguists en Inglaterra. Recientemente comenzó a interesarse por la traducción literaria, en especial la poesía. Ella tiene Licenciatura en Psicología de la University of Bolton, y está realizando su posgrado como maestra de español a nivel secundaria *con* Qualified Teacher Status en Birmingham City.

Miguel Ángel Albújar es un escritor barcelonés afincado en América. Le interesa la ciencia ficción y la fantasía, especialmente la fantástica política ficción que todo lo aguanta. Vive con su mujer y su ejército de suculentas.

Seila Benavente Miranda was born in Asturias, Spain, where she graduated in Psychology and Education Sciences. Since 2007 she teaches Spanish Language at the University of South Carolina, in Columbia. She started writing poetry when young and published several poems in Spain in the 1990s, but it is not until 2020 that she has her first published book *He venido a amarte*. It is a compilation of poems that talks about the pain of deeply rooted feelings of love and loss, surrounded by images of the earthy and coastal landscape of Asturias, always present. Accompanying her poetic oeuvre is her artistic passion for painting. She has been devoted for the last years to experimenting and developing new venues in painting, ranging from realistic to abstract. That is the holistic approach to life that combines the art with the education of the minds, that she is firmly engaged in.

Jesús Cortez is an undocumented writer and poet from West Anaheim, California. His work is inspired by his upbringing by a single Guerrerence mother during the 1990's. Through his works, he hopes to shed light on the people and stories about the city that tend to be ignored by the mainstream. His work has appeared in *The Acentos Review*, *Harvard Palabritas*, and *Dryland Literary Journal*, among other publications.

LR Cunningham is a poet, translator, and Assistant Professor of Spanish focusing on Hemispheric Studies and the Environment. In addition to *Contrapuntos*, her work has appeared in publications such as *Plants & Poetry Review*, *ABC-Clio*, *Stonecoast Review*, and *Oberon Magazine*, amongst others.

Theo Czajkowski creció en el estado de Michigan, Estados Unidos, y vive en México. Sus cuentos más recientes se han publicado en *Terrain*, *Panorama Journal*, y *Arboreal Literary Magazine*, entre otros.

Brandi DeHaven is a student attending and working at the University of South Carolina Aiken. She discovered writing as a creative outlet in her youth when reading Rohl Dahl's *The Witches*. She admired how immersive the experience of reading can be. Apart from reading she also focuses on her studies, her on campus job, and her military career. For Brandi, poetry is the most concise form of storytelling that she utilizes when life happens too fast and must be captured.

Rachel Eubanks is in her junior year at the University of South Carolina at Aiken earning her bachelor's degree in English and Psychology. She has received the Washington Writer's Award for Poetry, the Virginia Kaplan Award, and the Dr. Ellen Lott Smith Endowed Scholarship for her writing. She is a part-time tutor for her university's Writing Center. She is currently composing an electroencephalograph study to investigate the impact of emotional invalidation in childhood on emotional regulation.

Jonathan Ferrini is a published author who resides in San Diego. A partial collection of his stories is included within *Hearts Without Sleeves. Twenty-Three Stories* available on Amazon. Jonathan received his MFA in motion picture and television production from UCLA: "I'm proud to write from the perspective of diverse protagonists navigating life within dramatic and romantic storylines".

Colin Ian Jeffery is an English poet of the modernist movement with development of imagism stressing clarity, precision and economy of language, and has a strong reaction against war, tranny, and oppression of truth and innocence, but unlike other poets in the modernist movement like Dylan Thomas and Ezra Pound he has a profound faith in God.

Michael Manerowski's writing has seen publication in *Laurel Review*, *The Briar Cliff Review*, *The Alembic*, *2River*, *I-70 Review*, *The Thieving Magpie*, and is forthcoming in *Rundelania* and *Wilderness House Literary Review*. He holds an MFA in Creative Writing from Hamline University.

Jorge Manzanilla Pérez es estudiante del doctorado en Estudios Culturales por la Universidad de Arizona, Maestro en Escritura Creativa por la Universidad de El Paso Texas y Licenciado en Literatura Hispanoamericana por la Universidad Autónoma de Guerrero, ha publicado los siguientes libros de poesía: *Escarnio*, *Diáfano 23* y *Vitral de todos mis cuerpos*. Fue acreedor a la mención honorífica en el Premio Internacional de Poesía Ciudad de Mérida 2015. En El Paso, Texas obtuvo el galardón Creative Awards 2017. Obra suya se ha publicado en el *New York Times* y se ha traducido al portugués. Actualmente se enfoca en estudios del comic político en México.

Michael McGuire was born and raised and has lived in or near much of his life; his horse is nondescript, his dog is dead. Naturally, McGuire regrets not having passed his life in academia, for the alternative has proven somewhat varied, even unpredictable.

María Mínguez Arias es la autora de la novela *Patricia sigue aquí* (Editorial Egales, 2018). Su libro *Nombrar el cuerpo* (Editorial Egales y El BeiSmAn PrESs, septiembre 2022) es un híbrido entre crónica personal y exploración feminista y queer en el que reflexiona sobre el cuerpo de la mujer a partir de su propio cuerpo enfermo y disidente. Sus relatos y ensayos aparecen en las antologías Vol. 2 FIL Ciudad de Nueva York (CUNY Academic Works, próximamente), *Enviado Especial* (SEd, 2022), *Asintomática* (Hypermedia, 2021), *Los otros exilios* (Editorial Salta Pa'trás, 2021), *Locas y perversas* (Editorial Egales, 2020), *El cuento, por favor* (Ediciones Fuentetaja, 2007); y en las revistas *El BeiSmAn*, *Revista Hostosiana*, *riverSedge*, *Rio Grande Review* y próximamente, *Sinister Wisdom*. Además, es co-editora de la antología de narrativa escrita por mujeres en Estados Unidos, *#NiLocasNiSolas* (El BeiSmAn PrESs, 2022), y miembro del Consejo Editorial de la revista *El BeiSmAn: Literatura en español de Estados Unidos*. Mínguez Arias trabaja como directora de operaciones en la editorial feminista Aunt Lute Books en la Bahía de San Francisco donde reside con su compañera e hijes.

Ani Palacios es una escritora y periodista peruana que emigró a los Estados Unidos en 1988. Dirige Pukiyari Editores y Contacto Latino. Conduce el podcast Primera Persona. Organiza concursos literarios. Ha ganado doce International Latino Book Awards, cuatro de ellos primer puesto por mejor novela. Sus novelas incluyen: *Nos vemos en Purgatorio, Plumbago Torres y el sueño americano, 99 Amaneceres, Noche de Penas, El último clóset, Paloma aventurera, Hay un muerto en mi balcón, Los amantes de la viuda Cuevas, Heridas pendientes*. No ficción: *No Strings Attached: Your Journey to Unconditional Loving* y *Living in a Double World: A Practical Guided Tour Through the Immigration Experience*. Sus relatos aparecen en diversas antologías. Ha presentado en conferencias, talleres y ferias del libro; fundó la Sociedad de Escritores de Columbus; organizó FIL Ohio 2017 y 2018; fue reconocida en Who is Who in Columbus Latino y recibió el Premio Mi Gente por su trabajo con la literatura latina. Pertenece a la delegación de Indiana de la ANLE. Su historia es capturada en How They Made It in America.

Lisandra Pérez es una poeta que vive cerca de las vías del tren en Chicago. Lisandra es Editora de Poesía de *Passages North*, y sus palabras han sido publicadas en *The Acentos Review, Heavy Feather Review*, y otros. Siempre usa zapatos crocs y disfruta del pasatiempo de pasar la aspiradora. Encuentra a Lisandra en la Plataforma X @perezlisandra_.

Marcos Pico Rentería (México, 1981) es profesor asistente de español en Defense Language Institute. Su investigación se centra en literatura latinoamericana, principalmente en torno al desarrollo del cuento y ensayo en la producción mexicana de la segunda mitad del siglo XX y comienzos del XXI. En cuanto a sus intereses principales se encuentra el grupo literario mexicano Crack y el comienzo ensayístico de Jorge Volpi. Fue editor de *Nueve délficos. Ensayos sobre Lezama* (2014) publicado por la editorial Verbum (Madrid). Varios de sus cuentos, entrevistas, artículos y poemas han aparecido en revistas literarias y académicas como *Conexos, La Santa Crítica, Revista Crítica, Nuestra Aparente Rendición, Eñe: Revista para leer, Vozed, Digo.palabra.txt,*

Confluencia, *Caleidoscopio*, *Campos de Plumas*, *Carátula* y en antologías como *Alebrije de palabras* (BUAP, 2013), *Pelota Jara* (2014), *Testigos de Ausencias* (2018), *Hostos Review* (2019), entre otras.

Carlos Ponce-Meléndez poems have appeared in *The Dreamcatcher*, *The Poet*, *Voices Along the River*, *Desahogate*, *Small Brushes*, *The Texas Observer*, *El Angel*, *Celebrate*, several anthologies and numerous Spanish magazines. He also teaches creative writing at schools and community centers.

Ángel M. Rañales (A Coruña, 1992) es profesor de español, literatura hispánica y estudios ibéricos en la Universidad de Carolina del Sur Aiken, donde compagina su profesión con la edición, la lectura variopinta y el cuidado de sus plantas. Anteriormente residió en Lawrence, Kansas, donde cursó su maestría y doctorado, y en Santiago de Compostela, España, donde descubrió su amor por los libros y las letras que actualmente lo mantienen felizmente ocupado.

Jennifer Rathbun es poeta y traductora, profesora de español y directora del departamento de lenguas en Ball State University en Indiana. Recibió su doctorado de la Universidad de Arizona con especialización en Letras Latinoamericanas Contemporáneas. Es traductora de dieciséis poemarios de autores hispanos como Alberto Blanco y Minerva Margarita Villarreal, editora de dos antologías de poesía y autora del poemario *El libro de traiciones | The Book of Betrayals* (2021). Rathbun ganó el Premio Ambroggio 2021 otorgado por La Academia de Poetas Americanos por su traducción del poemario *Cardenal en mi ventana con una máscara en su pico* del autor colombiano Carlos Aguasaco. Es miembro de la Asociación Literaria de Traductores Literarios (ALTA) y editora de Ashland Poetry Press.

Cristina Rentería Garita (Puebla, México, 1980). Es Doctora en Economía, Sociología y Política Agraria por la Universidad de Córdoba (España) y Doctora en Educación (Didáctica y Lengua de la Literatura) por la Universidad de Almería (España). En 2018 obtuvo la Mención Honorífica en el Premio Nacional Dolores Castro por su proyecto "Oír con los Ojos, Estampas de la violencia en México" (Aguascalientes, México). En 2020, publicó su primera obra, *Juan y los Murmullos*

(Ediciones Azimut, Málaga, España), finalista al Premio Andalucía de la Crítica 2021. En 2021, además, fue finalista del Premio Ucopoética (Córdoba, España), dirigido a la poesía emergente. Es posible seguir su carrera literaria en www.paranarrar.com o en Instagram @renteriagarita.

Andrea Zelaya is a scholar, educator, writer, and translator. She is currently a PhD candidate in the Department of Literature at the University of California, San Diego. She received her MA in Literature from the University of California, San Diego and her BA in both English and Spanish Literature from Texas A&M University-Corpus Christi with minors in Latin American Studies and History, as well as a TESOL certification. As a Central American immigrant, her cultural heritage and background inform her creative, academic, and social justice endeavors. She has served as a pro bono translator for various non-profit organizations and immigrant communities in South Texas. Currently, her creative work and research focus on trauma and memory in postwar Central America and contemporary Central American migration experiences in the U.S. She has published fiction and poetry in English and Spanish.

DIGITUS INDIE PUBLISHERS
www.digitusindie.com
EDITORES INDEPENDIENTES